PENGUIN BOOKS

THE PERFECT NANNY

Leila Slimani is the first Moroccan woman to win France's most prestigious literary prize, the Goncourt, which she won for *The Perfect Nanny*. A journalist, she was born in Rabat, Morocco, in 1981. Her first novel, *The Ogre's Garden*, won the Prix La Mamounia. Slimani lives in Paris with her French husband and their two young children.

THE
PERFECT
NANNY

A Novel

LEILA SLIMANI

Translated from the French by
SAM TAYLOR

PENGUIN BOOKS

PENGUIN BOOKS
An imprint of Penguin Random House LLC
375 Hudson Street
New York, New York 10014
penguin.com

Originally published in French as *Chanson Douce* by Editions Gallimard, Paris.

LIBRARY OF CONGRESS CATALOGING-IN-PUBLICATION DATA
Names: Slimani, Leila, 1981– author.
Title: The perfect nanny : a novel / Leila Slimani.
Other titles: *Chanson douce*. English
Description: New York : Penguin Books, 2018.
Identifiers: LCCN 2017038080 (print) | LCCN 2017046748 (ebook) |
ISBN 9780525503897 (ebook) | ISBN 9780143132172 (paperback)
Subjects: | BISAC: FICTION / Contemporary Women. | Fiction / Literary.
Classification: LCC PQ2719.L56 (ebook) | LCC PQ2719.L56 C4313 2018
(print) | DDC 843/.92—dc233
LC record available at https://lccn.loc.gov/2017038080

Printed in the United States of America
3 5 7 9 10 8 6 4

Set in Aldus Nova
Designed by Sabrina Bowers

for Émile

Miss Vezzis came from across the Borderline to look after some children who belonged to a lady until a regularly ordained nurse could come out. The lady said Miss Vezzis was a bad, dirty nurse, and inattentive. It never struck her that Miss Vezzis had her own life to lead and her own affairs to worry over, and that these affairs were the most important things in the world to Miss Vezzis.

—Kipling, *Plain Tales from the Hills*

"Do you understand, dear sir, do you understand what it means when there is absolutely nowhere to go?" Marmeladov's question of the previous day came suddenly into his mind. "For every man must have somewhere to go."

—Dostoevsky, *Crime and Punishment*

THE

PERFECT

NANNY

The baby is dead. It took only a few seconds. The doctor said he didn't suffer. The broken body, surrounded by toys, was put inside a gray bag, which they zipped shut. The little girl was still alive when the ambulance arrived. She'd fought like a wild animal. They found signs of a struggle, bits of skin under her soft fingernails. On the way to the hospital she was agitated, her body shaken by convulsions. Eyes bulging, she seemed to be gasping for air. Her throat was filled with blood. Her lungs had been punctured, her head smashed violently against the blue chest of drawers.

They photographed the crime scene. They dusted for fingerprints and measured the surface area of the bathroom and the children's bedroom. On the floor, the princess rug was soaked with blood. The changing table had been knocked sideways. The toys were put in transparent bags and sealed as evidence. Even the blue chest of drawers will be used in the trial.

The mother was in a state of shock. That was what the paramedics said, what the police repeated, what the journalists wrote. When she went into the room where the children lay, she let out a scream, a scream from deep within, the howl of a she-wolf. It made the walls tremble. Night fell on this May day. She vomited and that was how the police found her, squatting in the bedroom, her clothes soiled, shuddering like a madwoman. She screamed her lungs out. The ambulance man nodded discreetly and they picked her up, even though she resisted and kicked out at them. They lifted her slowly to her feet and the young female trainee paramedic administered a tranquilizer. It was her first month on the job.

They had to save the other one too, of course. With the same level of professionalism; without emotion. She didn't know how to die. She only knew how to give death. She had slashed both her wrists and stabbed the knife in her throat. She must have lost consciousness, lying next to the cot. They took her pulse and blood pressure. They moved her on to the stretcher and the young trainee applied pressure to the wound in her neck.

The neighbors have gathered outside the building. Women, mostly. It will soon be time to fetch their children from school. They stare at the ambulance, puffy-eyed. They cry and they want to know. They stand on tiptoe, trying to make out what is happening behind the police cordon, inside the ambulance as it sets off, sirens screaming. They whisper to one another. Already the rumor is spreading. Something terrible has happened to the children.

It is a handsome apartment building on Rue d'Hauteville, in Paris's tenth arrondissement. A building where neighbors offer friendly greetings, even if they don't know each other. The Massés' apartment is on the fifth floor. It's the smallest apartment in the building. Paul and Myriam built a dividing wall in the living room when their second child was born. They sleep in one half of that room, a cramped space between the kitchen and the window that overlooks the street. Myriam likes Berber rugs and furniture that she finds in antique stores. She has hung Japanese prints on the walls.

Today she came home early. She cut short a meeting and put off the examination of a dossier until tomorrow. Sitting on a folding seat on a Line 7 train, she thought about how she would surprise her children. During the short walk from the metro station, she stopped at a baker's. She bought a baguette, a dessert for the little ones and an orange cake for the nanny. Her favorite.

She thought about taking the children to the fairground rides. After that, they would buy the food for dinner together. Mila would ask for a toy, Adam would suck on a crust of bread in his stroller.

Adam is dead. Mila will be too, soon.

"No illegal immigrants, agreed? For a cleaning lady or a decorator, it doesn't bother me. Those people have to work, after all. But to look after the little ones, it's too dangerous. I don't want someone who'd be afraid to call the police or go to the hospital if there was a problem. Apart from that . . . not too old, no veils and no smokers. The important thing is that she's energetic and available. That she works so we can work." Paul has prepared everything. He's drawn up a list of questions and scheduled thirty minutes for each interview. They have set aside their Saturday afternoon to find a nanny for their children.

A few days before this, Myriam was discussing her search with her friend Emma, who complained about the woman that looked after her boys. "The nanny has two sons here, so she can never stay late or babysit for us. It's really not practical. Think about that when you do your interviews. If she has children, it'd be better if they're back in her homeland." Myriam thanked her for the advice. But, in reality, what Emma said had upset her. If an employer had spoken about her or one of her friends in that way, she would have cried discrimination. To her, the idea of ruling a woman out of a job because she has children is terrible. She prefers not to bring the subject up with Paul. Her husband is like Emma. Pragmatic. Someone who places his family and his career above all else.

That morning, they went to the market together, all four of them. Mila on Paul's shoulders, Adam asleep in his stroller. They bought flowers and now they are tidying up the apartment. They want to make a good impression on the nannies who will come here. They pick up the books and magazines that litter the floor around and under their bed, and even in the bathroom. Paul asks Mila to put her toys away in large plastic trays. The little girl refuses, whining, and in the end he piles them up against the wall. They fold the children's clothes, change the sheets on the beds. They clean, throw stuff away, try desperately to air this stifling apartment. They want the nannies to see that they are good people; serious, orderly people who try to give their children the best of everything. The nannies must understand that Myriam and Paul are the ones in charge here.

Mila and Adam take a nap. Myriam and Paul sit on the edge of their bed. Anxious, uncomfortable. They have never entrusted their children to anyone before. Myriam was in her last year at law school when she became pregnant with Mila. She graduated two weeks before the birth. Paul was getting more and more work placements, full of that optimism that had drawn Myriam to him when they first met. He was sure he'd earn enough money for both of them. Certain that, despite the financial crisis, despite budget restrictions, he would forge a career in the music industry.

Mila was a fragile, irritable baby who cried constantly. She didn't put on weight, refusing her mother's breast and the bottles that her father prepared. Leaning over the crib, Myriam forgot that the outside world even existed. Her ambitions were limited to persuading this puny, bawling infant to swallow a few ounces of milk. Months passed without her even realizing. Paul and she were never separated from Mila. They pretended not to notice as their friends got annoyed, whispering behind their backs that a baby has no place in a bar or a restaurant. But Myriam absolutely refused to consider using a babysitter. She alone was capable of meeting her daughter's needs.

Mila was barely eighteen months old when Myriam became pregnant again. She always claimed it was an accident. "The pill is never a hundred percent," she told her friends, laughing. In reality, that pregnancy was premeditated. Adam was an excuse not to leave the sweetness of home. Paul did not express any reservations. He'd just been hired as an assistant in a famous studio, where he spent his days and nights, a hostage to the whims of the artists and their schedules. His wife seemed to be blooming; a natural mother. This cocooned existence, far from the world and other people, protected them from everything.

And then time started to drag; the clocklike perfection of the family mechanism became jammed. Paul's parents, who had got into a routine of helping them after Mila's birth, began to spend more and more time at their house in the country, where they were carrying out major repairs. One month before Myriam's due date, they organized a three-week trip to Asia and didn't tell Paul until the last minute. He took offense, complaining to Myriam of his parents' selfishness, their irresponsibility. But Myriam was relieved. She couldn't stand having Sylvie under her feet. She would smile as she listened to her mother-in-law's advice; she would say nothing when she saw her rummaging inside the fridge, criticizing the food she found there. Sylvie bought organic salads. She made meals for Mila but left the kitchen in a disgusting mess. Myriam and Sylvie never saw eye to eye on anything, and the apartment was filled with a dense, simmering unease that threatened at any moment to break into open warfare. In the end Myriam told Paul: "Let your parents live their lives. They're right to make the most of their freedom."

She didn't realize the magnitude of the task she had taken on. With two children, everything became more complicated: shopping, bath time, housework, visits to the doctor. The bills piled up. Myriam became gloomy. She began to hate going to the park. The winter days seemed endless. Mila's tantrums drove her mad, Adam's first burblings left her indifferent. With each passing day, she felt more and more desperate to go out for a walk on her own. Sometimes she wanted to scream like a lunatic in the street. They're eating me alive, she would think.

She was jealous of her husband. In the evenings, she stood by the door in a frenzy of anticipation, waiting for him to come home. Then she would complain for an hour about the children's screaming, the size of the apartment, her lack of free time. When she let him talk and he told her about epic recording sessions with a hip-hop group, she would spit: "You're lucky." He would reply: "No, you're the lucky one. I would love to see them grow up." No one ever won when they played that game.

At night Paul lay beside her, sleeping the deep, heavy sleep of someone who has worked hard all day and deserves a good rest. Bitterness and regret ate away at her. She thought about the efforts she had made to finish her degree, despite the lack of money and parental support, the joy she had felt when she was called to the Bar, the first time she had worn her lawyer's robes and Paul had taken a picture of her, smiling proudly outside their apartment building.

For months she pretended she was okay. Even to Paul, she didn't dare admit her secret shame. How she felt as if she were dying because she had nothing to talk about but the antics of her children and the conversations of strangers overheard in the supermarket. She started turning down dinner invitations, ignoring calls from her friends. She was especially wary of women, who could be so cruel. She wanted to strangle the ones who pretended to admire or, worse, envy her. She couldn't bear listening to them anymore, complaining about their jobs, about not seeing their children enough. More than anything, she feared strangers. The ones who innocently asked what she did for a living and who looked away when she said she was a stay-at-home mother.

One day, after doing the shopping in Monoprix on Boulevard Saint-Denis, she realized that she had, without meaning to, stolen a pair of children's socks. She'd dropped them in the stroller and forgotten about them. She was a few yards from home and she could have gone back to the shop to return them, but she decided not to. She didn't tell Paul. It was not an interesting subject, and yet she couldn't stop thinking about it. After that incident, she would regularly go to Monoprix and hide things inside her son's stroller: some shampoo or lotion or a lipstick that she would never use. She knew perfectly well that, if the security guards stopped her, she would just have to play the part of a stressed-out mother and they would probably believe her. There was something hypnotic about those pathetic little thefts. Alone in the street sometimes, she would laugh with the feeling that she was taking the whole world for a ride.

When she bumped into Pascal one day, by chance, she saw it as a sign. Her former law-school classmate must not have recognized her at first: she was wearing trousers that were too big for her and an old pair of boots, and she'd tied her unwashed hair up in a bun. She was standing next to the merry-go-round, which Mila refused to come down from. "This is your last go," she repeated each time her daughter, gripping tightly on to a horse, passed her with a wave. She looked up: Pascal was smiling at her, arms outstretched to signify his joy and surprise. She smiled back, hands clinging to the stroller handle. Pascal didn't have much time, but, as luck would have it, his next meeting was close to where Myriam lived. "I have to go home anyway," she told him. "Shall we walk together?"

Myriam grabbed hold of Mila, who gave an ear-splitting scream. She refused to budge but Myriam stubbornly kept smiling, pretending that the situation was under control. She couldn't stop thinking about the old sweater she was wearing under her coat and how Pascal must have seen its frayed collar. She frantically rubbed at her temples, as if that were enough to neaten her dry, tangled hair. Pascal seemed oblivious to all this. He told her about the law firm he'd set up with two friends from their year, the difficulties and pleasures of starting his own business. She drank in his words. Mila kept interrupting and Myriam would have given anything to shut her up. Without breaking eye contact with Pascal, she searched in her pockets, in her bag, to find a lollipop, a candy, anything at all that might buy her daughter's silence.

Pascal barely glanced at the children. He did not ask their names. Even Adam, asleep in his stroller, his face peaceful and adorable, did not seem to have any effect on him.

"Here we are." Pascal kissed her on the cheek. He said, "I'm very glad I got to see you again," and he went into the building. The heavy blue door slammed shut, and Myriam jumped. She began to pray silently. There, in the street, she felt so desperate that she could have thrown herself to the ground and wept. She had wanted to hang on to Pascal's leg, to beg him to take her with him, to give her a chance. Walking home, she felt utterly dejected. She looked at Mila, who was playing calmly. She gave the baby a bath and thought to herself that this happiness—this simple, silent, prisonlike happiness—was not enough to console her. Pascal had probably made fun of her. Maybe he'd even called a few of their former classmates to tell them about Myriam's pathetic life and how she "has lost her looks" and "didn't have the brilliant career we all expected."

All night, imaginary conversations gnawed at her brain. The next day, she had just got out of the shower when she heard her phone buzz. A text from Pascal: "I don't know if you have any plans to become a lawyer again. But if you're interested, give me a call." Myriam almost howled with joy. She started jumping around the apartment and kissed Mila, who asked her: "What's going on, Mama? Why are you laughing?" Later Myriam wondered whether Pascal had sensed her despair or whether, quite simply, he couldn't believe his luck: bumping into Myriam Charfa, the most dedicated student he had ever met. Maybe he thought he was doubly blessed, to be able to hire a woman like her and to bring her back to the courtroom, where she belonged.

Myriam spoke to Paul about it and she was disappointed by his reaction. "I didn't know you wanted to work," he shrugged. That made her furious, more than it should have done. The conversation quickly descended into mud-slinging. She called him an egotist; he described her behavior as thoughtless. "You're going to work? Well, that's fine, but what are we going to do about the children?" he sneered, ridiculing her ambitions and reinforcing the impression she had that she was a prisoner in this apartment.

Once they had calmed down, they patiently studied their options. It was late January: there was no point hoping to find a place in day care. They didn't have any connections in the town hall. And if she did start working again, they would be in the worst of all worlds: too rich to receive welfare and too poor to consider the cost of a nanny as anything other than a sacrifice. This, though, was the solution they chose in the end, after Paul said: "If you add in the extra hours, you and the nanny will earn more or less the same amount. But if you think it'll make you happy . . ." That conversation left a bitter taste in her mouth. She felt angry with Paul.

She wanted to do things right. To reassure herself, she went to a nearby agency that had just opened. A small office, simply decorated, run by two women in their early thirties. The shopfront was painted baby blue and adorned with little gold stars and camels. Myriam rang the bell. Through the window, the manager looked her up and down. She got slowly to her feet and poked her head through the half-open door.

"Yes?"

"Hello."

"Have you come to apply? We need a complete dossier. A curriculum vitae and references signed by your previous employers."

"No, not at all. I've come for my children. I'm looking for a nanny."

The woman's face was suddenly transformed. She seemed happy to welcome a customer and equally embarrassed by the contempt she had shown. But how could she have imagined that this tired-looking woman with her bushy, curly hair was the mother of the pretty little girl whining on the sidewalk?

The manager opened a large catalog and Myriam leaned over it. "Please, sit down," she said. Dozens of photographs of women, most of them African or Filipino, flashed past Myriam's eyes. Mila had fun looking at them all. She said: "That one's ugly, isn't she?" Her mother scolded her and, with a heavy heart, returned to those blurred, poorly framed portraits of unsmiling women.

The manager disgusted her. Her hypocrisy, her plump red face, the frayed scarf she wore around her neck. Her racism, so obvious just a minute ago. All this made Myriam want to run away. She shook the woman's hand. She promised she would speak to her husband about it and she never went back. Instead she pinned a small ad to noticeboards in various local shops. On the advice of a friend, she inundated websites with posts marked URGENT. By the end of the first week, they had received six calls.

She is awaiting this nanny as if she is the Savior, while at the same time she is terrified by the idea of leaving her children with someone else. She knows everything about them and would like to keep that knowledge secret. She knows their tastes, their habits. She can tell immediately if one of them is ill or sad. She has kept them close to her all this time, convinced that no one could protect them as well as she can.

Ever since her children were born, Myriam has been scared of everything. Above all, she is scared that they will die. She never talks about this—not to her friends, not to Paul—but she is sure that everyone has had the same thoughts. She is certain that, like her, they have watched their child sleep and wondered how they would feel if that little body were a corpse, if those eyes were closed forever. She can't help it. Her mind fills with horrible scenarios and she shakes her head to get rid of them, recites prayers, touches wood and the Hand of Fatima that she inherited from her mother. She wards off misfortune, illness, accidents, the perverted appetites of predators. At night, she dreams about Adam and Mila suddenly disappearing in the midst of an indifferent crowd. She yells, "Where are my children?" and the people laugh. They think she's crazy.

"She's late. Not a good start." Paul is growing impatient. He heads over to the front door and looks through the spyhole. It is 2:15 p.m. and the first applicant, a Filipino woman, still hasn't arrived.

At 2:20, Gigi knocks softly on the door. Myriam goes to open it. She notices immediately that the woman has very small feet. Despite the cold, she is wearing canvas trainers and white, frilly socks. Though nearly fifty years old, she has the feet of a child. She is quite elegant, her hair tied in a braid that falls halfway down her back. Paul coldly points out her lateness and Gigi lowers her head as she mumbles excuses. She expresses herself very poorly in French. Paul tentatively tries to interview her in English. Gigi talks about her experience. About her children, whom she left in her homeland; about the youngest one, whom she hasn't seen for ten years. Paul won't hire her. He asks a few token questions and at 2:30 he walks her to the door. "We'll call you. Thank you."

After that there is Grace, a smiling, undocumented immigrant from the Ivory Coast. Caroline, an obese blonde with dirty hair, who spends the interview complaining about her backache and her circulation problems. Malika, a Moroccan woman of a certain age, who stresses her twenty years of experience and her love of children. Myriam had been perfectly clear. She does not want to hire a North African to look after the children. "It'd be good," people told her. "Try to convince Paul. She could speak Arabic to them since you don't want to." But Myriam steadfastly refuses this idea. She fears that a tacit complicity and familiarity would grow between her and the nanny. That the woman would start speaking to her in Arabic. Telling Myriam her life story and, soon, asking her all sorts of favors in the name of their shared language and religion. She has always been wary of what she calls immigrant solidarity.

Then Louise arrived. When she describes that first interview, Myriam loves to say that it was instantly obvious. Like love at first sight. She goes on about the way her daughter behaved. "It was Mila who chose her," she likes to make clear. Mila had just woken from her nap, dragged from sleep by her brother's ear-splitting screams. Paul went to fetch the baby and came back with the little girl following close behind, hiding between his legs. Louise stood up. As Myriam describes this scene, she still sounds fascinated by the nanny's self-assurance. Louise delicately took Adam from his father's arms and pretended not to notice Mila. "Where is the princess? I thought I saw a princess, but she's disappeared." Mila burst out laughing and Louise continued with her game, searching in the corners, under the table, behind the sofa for the mysteriously vanished princess.

They ask her a few questions. Louise says that her husband is dead, that her daughter, Stéphanie, is grown-up now—"nearly twenty, I can hardly believe it"—and that she is always available. She gives Paul a piece of paper containing a list of her former employers. She talks about the Rouvier family, who are at the top of the list. "I stayed with them for a long time. They had two children too. Two boys." Paul and Myriam are charmed by Louise, by her smooth features, her open smile, her lips that do not tremble. She appears imperturbable. She looks like a woman able to understand and forgive everything. Her face is like a peaceful sea, its depths suspected by no one.

That evening they phoned the couple whose number Louise had given them. A woman answered, a little coldly. As soon as she heard Louise's name, her tone changed. "Louise? You're so lucky to have found her. She was like a second mother to my boys. It was heartbreaking when we had to let her go. To be perfectly honest, I even thought of having a third child at the time, just so we could keep her."

Louise opens the shutters of her apartment. It's just after five in the morning and, outside, the streetlamps are still lit. A man walks along the street, staying close to the walls to avoid the rain. The downpour lasted all night. The wind whistled in the pipes and invaded her dreams. The rain seems to be falling horizontally now so it can hit the building's facade and the windows with full force. Louise likes looking outside. Just across the road, between two sinister buildings, is a little house, surrounded by a bushy garden. A young Parisian couple moved there at the start of the summer, and on Sundays their children play on the swings and help weed the vegetable garden. Louise wonders what they're doing in this neighborhood.

She shivers from lack of sleep. With the tip of her fingernail she scratches the corner of the window. Even though she cleans it zealously twice a week, the glass always looks murky to her, covered in dust and black smears. Sometimes she wants to clean the panes until they shatter. She scratches, harder and harder, with her index finger, and her nail breaks. She puts her finger under water and bites it to stop the bleeding.

The apartment consists of only one room, which Louise uses as both bedroom and living room. She takes care, every morning, to fold up the sofa bed and put the black slipcover on it. She eats her meals at the coffee table, with the television on. Against the wall are piled some cardboard boxes. They contain perhaps the few objects that might give life to this soulless studio flat. To the right of the sofa is the photograph of a red-headed teenager in a sparkly frame.

She has carefully spread out her long skirt and blouse over the sofa. She picks up the ballet pumps that she left on the floor, a pair she bought more than ten years ago but which she's taken such good care of that they still look new. They are patent leather shoes, very simple, with square heels and a discreet little bow on top. She sits down and starts cleaning one, soaking a piece of cotton wool in a pot of makeup remover. Her movements are slow and precise. She cleans with furious care, completely absorbed in her task. The cotton wool is covered in grime. Louise brings the shoe over to the lamp placed on the pedestal table. When she is satisfied with the leather's shine, she puts the shoe down and picks up the second one.

It's so early that she has time to fix the fingernails she broke when she was cleaning. She wraps a plaster around her index finger and paints the other nails with a very discreet pink polish. For the first time, and despite the price, she had her hair dyed at the salon. She ties it in a bun, off her neck. She puts on her makeup and the blue eyeshadow makes her look older. She is so fragile, so slender, that from a distance you would think her barely out of her teens. In fact, she is over forty.

She paces around the room, which seems smaller, more cramped than ever. She sits down then stands up again almost immediately. She could turn on the television. Drink some tea. Read an old copy of the women's magazine that she keeps near her bed. But she is afraid of relaxing, letting the time slip past, surrendering to drowsiness. Waking up so early has left her weak, vulnerable. It wouldn't take much to make her close her eyes for a minute, and then she might fall asleep and she'd be late. She has to keep her mind alert, has to focus all her attention on this first day of work.

She can't wait at home. It's not even six yet—she's going to be much too early—but she walks quickly to the Saint-Maur-des-Fossés suburban train station. It takes her more than a quarter of an hour to get there. Inside the carriage, she sits opposite an old Chinese man, who sleeps curled up, with his forehead pressed against the window. She stares at his exhausted face. At each station, she thinks about waking him. She is afraid that he will be lost, go too far, that he will open his eyes, alone, at the terminus, and that he'll have to double back the way he came. But she doesn't say anything. It is more sensible not to speak to people. Once, a young girl, dark-haired and very beautiful, had almost slapped her. "What are you looking at? Eh? Why the hell are you staring at me?" she yelled.

When she arrives at the Auber station, Louise jumps down on to the platform. It's starting to get busy. A woman bumps into her while she is climbing down the stairs to the metro platform. She chokes on a sickening smell of croissant and burned chocolate. After taking Line 7 toward Opéra, she gets off at the Poissonnière station.

Louise is almost an hour early so she sits at a table on the terrace of the Paradis, a charmless café with a view of the building's entrance. She plays with her spoon. She casts envious glances at the man to her right, who sucks his cigarette with his thick-lipped lecher's mouth. She would like to grab it from his hand and take a long drag. Unable to stand it any longer, she pays her bill and goes into the silent building. She decides to ring the doorbell in a quarter of an hour, and in the meantime she waits on a step between two floors. She hears a noise and barely has time to get to her feet: it's Paul, hurtling downstairs. He's carrying his bike and wearing a pink helmet.

"Louise? Have you been here long? Why didn't you come in?"

"I didn't want to disturb you."

"You wouldn't disturb us. On the contrary! Here, these are your keys," he says, taking a bunch from his pocket. "Go ahead, make yourself at home."

"My nanny is a miracle-worker." That is what Myriam says when she describes Louise's sudden entrance into their lives. She must have magical powers to have transformed this stifling, cramped apartment into a calm, light-filled place. Louise has pushed back the walls. She has made the cupboards deeper, the drawers wider. She has let the sun in.

On the first day, Myriam gives her a few instructions. She shows her how the appliances work. Pointing to an object or a piece of clothing, she repeats: "Be careful with that. I'm very attached to it." She makes recommendations about Paul's vinyl collection, which the children must not touch. Louise nods, silent and docile. She observes each room with the self-assurance of a general standing before a territory he is about to conquer.

In the weeks that follow her arrival, Louise turns this hasty sketch of an apartment into an ideal bourgeois interior. She imposes her old-fashioned manners, her taste for perfection. Myriam and Paul can't get over it. She sews the buttons back on to jackets that they haven't worn for months because they've been too lazy to look for a needle. She hems skirts and pairs of trousers. She mends Mila's clothes, which Myriam was about to throw out without a qualm. Louise washes the curtains yellowed by tobacco and dust. Once a week, she changes the sheets. Paul and Myriam are overjoyed. Paul tells her with a smile that she is like Mary Poppins. He isn't sure she understands the compliment.

At night, in the comfort of their clean sheets, the couple laughs, incredulous at their new life. They feel as if they have found a rare pearl, as if they've been blessed. Of course, Louise's wages are a burden on the family budget, but Paul no longer complains about that. In a few weeks, Louise's presence has become indispensable.

When Myriam gets back from work in the evenings, she finds dinner ready. The children are calm and clean, not a hair out of place. Louise arouses and fulfills the fantasies of an idyllic family life that Myriam guiltily nurses. She teaches Mila to tidy up behind herself and her parents watch dumbstruck as the little girl hangs her coat on the peg.

Useless objects have disappeared. With Louise, nothing accumulates anymore: no dirty dishes, no dirty laundry, no unopened envelopes found later under an old magazine. Nothing rots, nothing expires. Louise never neglects anything. Louise is scrupulous. She writes everything down in a little flower-covered notebook. The times of the dance class, school outings, doctor's appointments. She copies the names of the medicines the children take, the price of the ice creams she bought for them at the fairground, and the exact words that Mila's schoolteacher said to her.

After a few weeks, she no longer hesitates to move objects around. She empties the cupboards completely, hangs little bags of lavender between the coats. She makes bouquets of flowers. She feels a serene contentment when—with Adam asleep and Mila at school—she can sit down and contemplate her task. The silent apartment is completely under her power, like an enemy begging for forgiveness.

But it's in the kitchen that she accomplishes the most extraordinary wonders. Myriam has admitted to her that she doesn't know how to cook anything and doesn't really want to learn. The nanny prepares meals that Paul goes into raptures about and the children devour, without a word and without anyone having to order them to finish their plate. Myriam and Paul start inviting friends again, and they are fed on *blanquette de veau*, *pot-au-feu*, ham hock with sage and delicious vegetables, all lovingly cooked by Louise. They congratulate Myriam, shower her with compliments, but she always admits: "My nanny did it all."

When Mila is at school, Louise attaches Adam to her in a large wrap. She likes to feel the child's chubby thighs against her belly, his saliva that runs down her neck when he falls asleep. She sings all day for this baby, praising him for his laziness. She massages him, taking pride in his folds of flesh, his round pink cheeks. In the mornings, the child welcomes her with gurgles, his plump arms reaching out for her. In the weeks that follow Louise's arrival, Adam learns to walk. And this boy who used to cry every night sleeps peacefully until morning.

Mila is wilder. She is a small, fragile girl with the posture of a ballerina. Louise ties her hair in buns so tight that the girl's eyes look slanted, pulled toward her temples. Like that, she resembles one of those medieval heroines with a broad forehead, a cold and noble expression. Mila is a difficult, exhausting child. Any time she becomes irritated, she screams. She throws herself to the ground in the middle of the street, stamps her feet, lets herself be dragged along to humiliate Louise. When the nanny crouches down and tries to speak to her, Mila turns away.

She counts out loud the butterflies on the wallpaper. She watches herself in the mirror when she cries. This child is obsessed by her own reflection. In the street, her eyes are riveted to shop windows. On several occasions she has bumped into lampposts or tripped over small obstacles on the sidewalk, distracted by the contemplation of her own image.

Mila is cunning. She knows that crowds stare, and that Louise feels ashamed in the street. The nanny gives in more quickly when they are in public. Louise has to take detours to avoid the toyshop on the avenue, where the little girl stands in front of the window and screams. On the way to school, Mila drags her feet. She steals a raspberry from a greengrocer's stall. She climbs on to windowsills, hides in porches, and runs away as fast as her legs will carry her. Louise tries to go after her while pushing the stroller, yelling the girl's name, but Mila doesn't stop until she comes to the very end of the sidewalk. Sometimes Mila regrets her bad behavior. She worries about Louise's paleness and the frights she gives her. She becomes loving again, cuddly. She makes it up to the nanny, clinging to her legs. She cries and wants to be mothered.

Slowly, Louise tames the child. Day after day, she tells her stories, where the same characters always recur. Orphans, lost little girls, princesses kept as prisoners, and castles abandoned by terrible ogres. Strange beasts—birds with twisted beaks, one-legged bears and melancholic unicorns—populate Louise's landscapes. The little girl falls silent. She stays close to the nanny, attentive, impatient. She asks for certain characters to come back. Where do these stories come from? They emanate from Louise, in a continual flood, without her even thinking about it, without her making the slightest effort of memory or imagination. But in what black lake, in what deep forest has she found these cruel tales where the heroes die at the end, after first saving the world?

Myriam is always disappointed when she hears the door open in the law firm where she works. Around 9:30 a.m., her colleagues start to arrive. They pour themselves coffee, telephones wail, the floorboards creak, the morning calm is shattered.

Myriam gets to the office before eight. She is always the first there. She turns on her desk lamp, nothing else. Beneath that halo of light, in that cave-like silence, she rediscovers the concentration she used to have in her student years. She forgets everything and plunges with relish into the examination of her dossiers. Sometimes she walks through the dark corridor, document in hand, and talks to herself. She smokes a cigarette on the balcony as she drinks her coffee.

The day she started work again, Myriam woke up at the crack of dawn, filled with a childlike excitement. She put on a new skirt, high heels, and Louise exclaimed: "You're very beautiful." On the doorstep, holding Adam in her arms, the nanny pushed her boss out the door. "Don't worry about us," she repeated. "Everything will be fine here."

Pascal gave Myriam a warm welcome. He assigned her the office next to his, with a communicating door that he often left ajar. Only two or three weeks after her arrival, Pascal entrusted her with responsibilities that some of his older employees had never been given. As the months passed, Myriam handled dozens of clients' cases on her own. Pascal encourages her to try her hand at everything and to use her capacity for hard work, which he knows to be immense. She never says no. She does not refuse any of the dossiers that Pascal hands to her, she never complains about working late. Pascal often tells her: "You're perfect." For months, she is weighed down by a mass of small cases. She defends sleazy dealers, halfwits, an exhibitionist, talentless robbers, alcoholics arrested at the wheel. She deals with cases of unpaid debt, credit-card fraud, identity theft.

Pascal counts on her to find him new clients and encourages her to devote her time to legal-aid cases. Twice a month she goes to the Bobigny court and waits in the corridor until 9 p.m. for verdicts to be handed down, eyes glued to her watch, the hands barely moving. Sometimes she gets annoyed, responding brusquely to her disoriented clients. But she gives her all and obtains the best possible deals. Pascal repeats to her constantly: "You have to know each dossier by heart." She takes him at his word. She rereads statements and reports until late at night. She picks out the slightest inaccuracy, spots the smallest procedural error. She works with a fury and in the end she earns her reward. Former clients recommend her to friends. Her name circulates among the prisoners. One young man, who avoided a prison sentence thanks to her, promises to pay her back. "You got me out of there. I won't forget that."

Once, she was called in the middle of the night and asked to report to the police station. A former client had been arrested for domestic violence. And yet he'd sworn to her that he was incapable of hitting a woman. She got dressed in the dark, soundlessly, at two in the morning, and she leaned down to kiss Paul. He grunted and then turned over.

Often her husband tells her that she is working too hard and that drives her crazy. He is offended by her reaction and makes a big show of his benevolence. He pretends to be concerned about her health, to worry that Pascal is exploiting her. She tries not to think about her children, not to let the guilt eat away at her. Sometimes she starts imagining that they are all in league against her. Her mother-in-law tries to persuade her that "if Mila is often ill, it's because she feels lonely." Her colleagues never invite her to go for a drink with them after work and are surprised whenever she works until late. "But don't you have children?" Even the schoolteacher summoned her one morning to talk about a ridiculous incident between Mila and one of her classmates. When Myriam apologized for having missed the latest meetings and for having sent Louise in her place, the gray-haired teacher spread her hands. "If you only knew! It's the modern malaise. All these poor children are left to their own devices while both parents are obsessed by their careers. They're always running. You know what two words parents say most often to their children these days? 'Hurry up!' And of course, we pay the price for all this. The children take out their anxieties and their feelings of abandonment on us."

Myriam had desperately wanted to put the teacher in her place, but she'd been incapable of doing it. Was it because of that little chair, on which she sat uncomfortably, in this little classroom that smelled of paint and plasticine? The setting, the teacher's voice, all of this brought her forcefully back to her childhood, to that age of obedience and obligation. Myriam smiled. She stupidly thanked the woman and promised her that Mila would make progress. She didn't throw the old harpy's misogyny and moralizing back in her face, as she wanted to. She was too afraid that the gray-haired lady would take out her revenge on Mila.

Pascal seems to understand her rage, her vast hunger for recognition, for challenges that measure up to her abilities. Between her and Pascal, a battle begins, and both of them draw an ambiguous pleasure from it. He pushes her; she stands up to him. He exhausts her; she doesn't disappoint him. One evening he invites her to have a drink with him after work. "You've been with us for nearly six months. That's worth celebrating, don't you think?" They walk down the street in silence. He holds the door of the bar open for her and she smiles at him. They sit at the back of the room, on an upholstered bench. Pascal orders a bottle of white wine. They talk about one of their dossiers and then, very quickly, start reminiscing about their student years. The big party their friend Charlotte threw in her mansion in the eighteenth arrondissement. The panic attack, absolutely hilarious, that poor Céline suffered on the day of her orals. Myriam drinks fast and Pascal makes her laugh. She doesn't feel like going home. She would like to have no one she has to call, no one waiting up for her. But there's Paul. And there are the children.

A gently thrilling, lightly erotic tension burns her throat and her breasts. She runs her tongue over her lips. She wants something. For the first time in a long time, she feels a gratuitous, futile, selfish desire. A desire of her own. Although she loves Paul, her husband's body is weighed down by memories. When he penetrates her, it is her motherly womb that he enters, her heavy belly, where Paul's sperm has so often been accommodated. Her belly of folds and waves, where they built their house, where so many worries and joys flowered. Paul has massaged her swollen, purple legs. He has seen the blood spread over the sheets. Paul has held her hair back from her forehead while she's vomited, on her knees. He has heard her scream. He has wiped the sweat from her face covered with angiomas while she pushed. He has delivered her children from her body.

She had always refused the idea that her children could be an impediment to her success, to her freedom. Like an anchor that drags you to the bottom, that pulls the face of the drowned man into the mud. At first, the realization that she was wrong had plunged her into a profound sadness. She thought it unjust, terribly frustrating. She became aware that she could never live without feeling that she was incomplete, that she was doing things badly, sacrificing one part of her life for another. She had made a big deal out of this, refusing to renounce her dream of the ideal balance. Stubbornly thinking that everything was possible, that she could reach all her objectives, that she wouldn't end up bitter or exhausted. That she wouldn't play the role of a martyr or of the perfect mother.

Every day, or nearly every day, Myriam receives a notification from her friend Emma. She posts sepia portraits of her two blonde children on social media. Perfect children who play in a park and go to a school that will allow them to blossom, bringing out the gifts that she already senses in them. She gave them unpronounceable names, taken from Nordic mythology, whose meanings she enjoys explaining. Emma is beautiful too, in these photographs. Her husband never appears in any of them, eternally devoted to taking pictures of an ideal family to which he belongs only as a spectator. He does his best to enter the frame, though. That bohemian bourgeois man with his beard and natural wool pullovers, who puts on tight, uncomfortable trousers to go to work.

Myriam would never dare tell Emma this thought that fleetingly crosses her mind, this idea that is not cruel but shameful, and that she has as she observes Louise and her children. We will, all of us, only be happy, she thinks, when we don't need one another anymore. When we can live a life of our own, a life that belongs to us, that has nothing to do with anyone else. When we are free.

Myriam heads to the door and looks through the spyhole. Every five minutes she repeats: "They're late." She is making Mila nervous. Sitting on the edge of the sofa in her hideous taffeta dress, Mila has tears in her eyes. "You think they're not coming?"

"Of course they're coming," Louise answers. "Give them time to get here."

The preparations for Mila's birthday party have taken on ludicrous proportions. For the past two weeks, Louise has talked about nothing else. In the evenings, when Myriam comes home from work, exhausted, Louise shows her the party streamers she has made herself. In a hysterical voice, she describes the taffeta dress that she found in a boutique and that will, she feels sure, make Mila ecstatic. Several times, Myriam has had to force herself not to tell Louise to forget the whole thing. She is tired of these ridiculous preoccupations. Mila is so young! Myriam doesn't see the point in putting her daughter in a state like this. But Louise stares at her with her wide-open little eyes. Just look at Mila—she is giddy with happiness.

That's all that counts, the pleasure of this little princess, the wonderland of her birthday celebration. Myriam swallows her sarcastic response. She feels as if she's been caught in the wrong, and ends up promising that she will do her best to be there for the party.

Louise decided to hold it on a Wednesday afternoon, when the children are off school. She wanted to be sure that everyone would be in Paris, and available to come. Myriam went to work that morning, swearing that she would come back after lunch.

When she got home, early in the afternoon, she almost cried out in surprise. She didn't recognize her own apartment anymore. The living room was literally transformed, dripping with glitter, balloons, paper streamers. But most of all, the sofa had been removed to allow the children to play. Even the oak table, so heavy that they'd never moved it since their arrival, had been pushed to the other side of the room.

"But who moved the furniture? Did Paul help you?"

"No," Louise replies. "I did all that myself."

Myriam, incredulous, wants to laugh. It must be a joke, she thinks, observing the nanny's match-thin arms. Then she remembers that she has already been taken aback by Louise's strength. Once or twice, she was impressed by the way she picked up heavy, bulky parcels while carrying Adam in her arms. Concealed behind that frail, narrow physique, Louise has the power of a colossus.

All morning Louise blew up balloons, twisted them into the shapes of animals and stuck them all over the apartment, from the entrance hall to the kitchen drawers.

She made the birthday cake herself, an enormous red fruit charlotte covered with decorations.

Myriam regrets having taken the afternoon off. She would have been so much happier in the calm of her office. Her daughter's birthday party makes her anxious. She is afraid that the other children will be bored, impatient. She doesn't want to have to deal with the ones who fight or console the ones whose parents are late to pick them up. Chilling memories of her own childhood come back to her. She sees herself on a thick, white wool carpet, isolated from the group of little girls playing with a doll's tea set. She had let a piece of chocolate melt on the carpet and then she'd tried to hide her misdeed, which had only made things worse. Her host's mother had told her off in front of everyone.

Myriam holes up in her bedroom, closing the door and pretending to be absorbed in reading her emails. She knows that, as always, she can depend on Louise. The doorbell starts to ring. The living room swells with the noise of children. Louise has put music on. Myriam sneaks out of her room and watches the little guests, massed around the nanny. They spin around her, completely captivated. She has prepared songs and magic tricks. She disguises herself as they watch in disbelief and the children, who are not at all easy to deceive, know that she is one of their own. She is there, vibrant, joyful, teasing. She hums songs, makes animal noises. She even carries Mila and one of her friends on her back, and the other kids laugh until they cry, begging her to let them take part in the rodeo as well.

Myriam admires this ability that Louise has to really play. When she plays, she is animated by that omnipotence that only children possess. One evening, coming home, Myriam finds Louise lying on the floor, her face painted. On her cheeks and forehead are the thick black lines of a warrior's mask. She has made an Indian headdress out of crêpe paper. In the middle of the living room she has built a misshapen tepee out of a sheet, a broomstick and a chair. Standing in the half-open doorway, Myriam feels troubled. She watches Louise as she twists her body and makes wild noises, and she is horribly embarrassed. The nanny looks like she's drunk. That is the first thought that comes to mind. Seeing Myriam there, Louise stands up, red-faced and staggering. "I've got pins and needles," she explains. Adam is clinging to her calf and Louise laughs, with a laugh that still belongs to the imaginary world in which their game is taking place.

Perhaps, Myriam reassures herself, Louise is simply a child too. She takes very seriously the games she plays with Mila. For example, if they play cops and robbers,

Louise lets herself be locked up behind invisible bars. Sometimes she plays the forces of law and order and runs after Mila. Each time, she invents a precise geography that Mila has to memorize. She creates costumes and develops a scenario filled with plot twists. She prepares the set with meticulous care. Occasionally the little girl gets tired of this. "Come on, let's start!" she begs.

Myriam doesn't know this, but Louise's favorite game is hide-and-seek. Except that nobody counts and there are no rules. The game is based on the element of surprise. Without warning, Louise disappears. She nestles in a corner and lets the children search for her. She often chooses hiding places where she can continue to observe them. She hides under the bed or behind a door and doesn't move. She holds her breath.

And so Mila understands that the game has begun. She hollers like a mad girl and claps her hands. Adam follows her lead. He laughs so hard that he can hardly stand, and several times he falls on to his bottom. They call her name, but Louise does not respond. "Louise? Where are you?" "Watch out, Louise, we're coming, we're going to find you."

Louise says nothing. She does not come out of her hiding place, even when they scream, when they cry, when they fall into despair. Crouching in the shadows, she spies on Adam as he panics, lying on his back and sobbing. He doesn't understand. He calls out "Louise," swallowing the last syllable, snot dribbling over his lips, his cheeks purple with rage. Mila, too, ends up being scared. For a moment, they start to believe that Louise has really gone, that she has abandoned them in this apartment where night will soon fall, that they are alone and she will not come back. The anguish is unbearable and Mila begs the nanny. She says: "Louise, this isn't funny. Where are you?" The child becomes annoyed, stamps her feet. Louise waits. She watches them as if she's studying the death throes of a fish she's just caught, its gills bleeding, its body shaken by spasms. The fish wriggling on the bottom of the boat, sucking the air through its exhausted mouth, the fish that has no chance of surviving.

Then Mila starts uncovering the hiding places. She has realized that she must open doors, lift up curtains, squat down to look under the bed. But Louise is so slim that she always finds new lairs where she can take refuge. She crawls into the laundry basket, under Paul's desk, or to the back of a cupboard, where she covers herself with a blanket. Sometimes she hides in the shower cubicle, in the darkness of the bathroom. So, Mila searches in vain. She sobs and Louise remains motionless. The child's despair does not make her yield.

One day, Mila doesn't cry anymore. Louise is caught in her own trap. Mila stays silent, pacing around the hiding spot and pretending not to know that the nanny is there. She sits on the laundry basket and Louise feels as if she will suffocate. "Truce?" whispers the child.

But Louise doesn't want to surrender. She just sits there, knees pressed to her chin, not saying a word. The little girl's feet tap softly against the wicker laundry basket. "Louise, I know you're in there," she says, laughing. Suddenly Louise stands up, knocking Mila to the floor. Her head bangs against the bathroom tiles. Dazed, the child cries and then, seeing the triumphant, resuscitated

Louise standing above her, staring down at her from the heights of her victory, Mila's terror is transformed to hysterical joy. Adam runs to the bathroom and joins in the girls' jig of delight, the three of them giggling until they can hardly breathe.

STÉPHANIE

At eight years old, Stéphanie knew how to change a nappy and prepare a baby's bottle. Her movements were sure and her hand did not tremble as she slipped it under the fragile neck of a newborn and lifted it up from the cot. She knew they had to be laid down on their backs and never shaken. She gave them baths, holding them firmly by the shoulder. The screams and cries of babies, their laughter and their tears were the soundtrack to her memories as an only child. Adults were thrilled by the love she showed the little ones. They thought she was exceptionally maternal and devoted for such a young girl.

When Stéphanie was a child, her mother, Louise, ran a day care at home. Or rather in Jacques's home, as he always insisted on pointing out. In the mornings, the mothers dropped off their children. She remembers those women, rushed and sad, standing with their ears glued to the door. Louise taught her to listen for their anxious footsteps in the corridor of the apartment building. Some of them went back to work very soon after giving birth and they handed their tiny newborns over to Louise. They also gave her—in opaque bags that Louise put in the fridge—the milk they'd pumped during the night. Stéphanie remembers those little containers arrayed on the shelf of the fridge with the children's names written on them. One night she got up and opened the bag belonging to Jules, a red-faced baby whose sharp nails had scratched her cheek. She drank it all without pausing. She never forgot that taste of rotting melon, that sour taste which stayed in her mouth for days afterward.

On Saturday evenings she would sometimes accompany her mother to vast-seeming apartments where they would babysit. Beautiful, important women passed her in the corridor, leaving a lipstick trace on their children's cheeks. The men didn't like to wait in the living room, embarrassed by the presence of Louise and Stéphanie. They hopped up and down on their heels, smiling stupidly. They scolded their wives then helped them put their coats on. Before leaving, the woman would crouch down, balanced on her thin stilettos, and wipe the tears from her son's cheeks. "Don't cry anymore, my love. Louise is going to tell you a story and give you a hug. Aren't you, Louise?" Louise would nod. She held those children as they struggled and screamed that they wanted their mothers. Sometimes, Stéphanie hated them. She was horrified by the way they hit Louise, the way they talked to her like little tyrants.

While Louise put the children to bed, Stéphanie would rummage through drawers and in boxes left on pedestal tables. She pulled out photograph albums hidden under coffee tables. Louise cleaned everything. She did the washing-up and wiped the kitchen countertops with a sponge. She folded the clothes that madam had tossed on her bed before leaving, hesitating over which outfit to wear. "You don't have to do the washing-up," Stéphanie would repeat. "Come and sit with me." But Louise adored that. She adored observing the parents' delighted faces when they came home and realized that they'd had a free cleaning lady as well as a babysitter.

The Rouviers, for whom Louise worked for several years, took them to their country house. Louise worked and Stéphanie was on vacation. But she wasn't there, like the hosts' children, to sunbathe and stuff herself with fruit. She wasn't there to bend the rules, to stay up late and learn to ride a bicycle. If she was there, it was because no one knew what else to do with her. Her mother told her to be discreet, to play silently. Not to give the impression that she was taking advantage of the situation. "I know they said this was sort of our vacation too, but if you have too much fun they'll take it badly." At the table, she sat next to her mother, away from the hosts and their guests. She remembers that the other people talked and talked while she and her mother lowered their eyes and swallowed their meals in silence.

The Rouviers found it hard to deal with the little girl's presence. It embarrassed them; it was almost physical. They felt a shameful antipathy toward that dark-haired child, in her faded swimsuit, that clumsy child with her blank face. When she sat in the living room, next to little Hector and Tancrède, to watch television, the parents couldn't help feeling annoyed. They always ended up asking her to do them a favor—"Stéphanie, be a sweetie, go and fetch my glasses from the entrance hall"—or telling her that her mother was expecting her in the kitchen. Thankfully, Louise forbade her daughter from going near the pool, without the Rouviers even having to say anything.

On the second-to-last day of the vacation, Hector and Tancrède invited some neighbor kids to play with them on their brand-new trampoline. Stéphanie, who was hardly any older than the boys, did some impressive tricks. Some risky jumps and somersaults that brought shouts of enthusiasm from the other children. In the end Mrs. Rouvier asked Stéphanie to get down, to let the little ones play. She went over to her husband and, in a compassionate voice, said to him: "Maybe we shouldn't invite her again. I think it's too hard for her. It must be tough, seeing all the things she's not allowed to do." Her husband smiled with relief.

Myriam has been waiting for this evening all week long. She opens the front door of the apartment. Louise's handbag is on the armchair in the living room. She hears children's voices singing. A song about a green mouse and boats on the water, something turning and something floating. She moves forward on tiptoes. Louise is kneeling on the floor, leaning over the edge of the bath. Mila dunks the body of her Russian doll into the water and Adam claps his hands as he sings. Delicately, Louise picks up balls of foam and places them on the children's heads. They laugh at these hats that fly off when the nanny blows on them.

In the metro, on her way home, Myriam had felt as impatient as a lover. She hadn't seen her children all week and tonight she had promised herself she would devote herself entirely to them. Together, they would slip into the big bed. She would tickle them and kiss them, she would squeeze them against her until they were dizzy. Until they struggled.

Hidden behind the bathroom door, she watches them

and she takes a deep breath. She feels a frenzied need to feed on their skin, to plant kisses on their little hands, to hear their high-pitched voices calling "Mama." She feels suddenly sentimental. This is what it's like, being a mother. It makes her a bit silly sometimes. The most banal moments suddenly seem important. Her heart is stirred by the smallest things.

This week she came home late every night. Her children were already asleep and, after Louise left, she would sometimes lie nuzzled up to Mila, in her little bed, breathing in the delicious smell of her daughter's hair, a chemical odor of strawberries. Tonight she will allow them to do things that are normally forbidden. They will eat chocolate sandwiches under the covers. They will watch a cartoon and fall asleep late, all snuggled up. In the night she'll get a few kicks in the face and she'll sleep badly because she's so worried about Adam falling off the bed.

The children come out of the water and run, naked, into their mother's arms. Louise starts cleaning up the bathroom. She wipes the tub with a sponge and Myriam tells her: "Don't bother, there's no need. It's late already. You can go home. You must have had a tough day." Louise pretends not to hear. Squatting down, she continues scrubbing the edge of the bath and tidying up the toys that the children have tossed around.

Louise folds the towels. She empties the washing machine and makes the children's beds. She puts the sponge back in a kitchen cupboard and takes out a saucepan, which she puts on the stove. Helplessly, Myriam watches her work. She tries to reason with her. "I'll do it, don't worry." She tries to take the saucepan from her, but Louise grips the handle tightly in her palm. Gently, she pushes Myriam away. "Go and rest," she says. "You must be tired. Enjoy your children. I'll make their supper. You won't even see me."

And it's true. As the weeks pass, Louise becomes ever better at being simultaneously invisible and indispensable. Myriam no longer calls to warn her that she's going to be late and Mila no longer asks when Mama is coming home. Louise is there, single-handedly holding up this fragile edifice. Myriam lets herself be mothered. Every day she abandons more tasks to a grateful Louise. The nanny is like those figures at the back of a theater stage who move the sets around in the darkness. She picks up a couch, pushes a cardboard column or a wall with one hand. Louise works in the wings, discreet and powerful. She is the one who controls the transparent wires without which the magic cannot occur. She is Vishnu, the nurturing divinity, jealous and protective; the she-wolf at whose breast they drink, the infallible source of their family happiness.

You look at her and you do not see her. Her presence is intimate but never familiar. She arrives earlier and earlier, leaves later and later. One morning, coming out of the shower, Myriam finds herself naked in front of the nanny, who does not even blink. "Why should she care about my body?" Myriam reassures herself. "She's not prudish like that."

Louise encourages the couple to go out. "You should make the most of your youth," she repeats mechanically.

Myriam listens to her advice. She thinks Louise wise and kindly. One evening Paul and Myriam go to a party thrown by a musician whom Paul has just met. The musician lives in an attic apartment in the sixth arrondissement. The living room is tiny and low-ceilinged, and the guests are crammed close together. There's a very happy atmosphere and soon everyone starts dancing. The musician's wife—a tall blonde with fuchsia lipstick—passes around joints and pours shots of vodka into ice-cold glasses. Myriam doesn't know these people at all, but she talks with them and laughs loudly, her head thrown back. She spends an hour in the kitchen, sitting on the countertop. At three in the morning, the guests say they're starving and the beautiful blonde makes a mushroom omelet that they eat bent over the frying pan, their forks clinking.

When they go home, about 4 a.m., Louise is dozing on the sofa, her legs folded up under her chest, hands joined together. Paul delicately spreads a blanket over her. "Don't wake her up. She looks so peaceful." And Louise starts sleeping there, once or twice a week. It's never clearly stated—they don't talk about it—but Louise patiently builds her nest in the middle of the apartment.

At times, Paul worries about the nanny's long hours. "I don't want her to accuse us of exploiting her one day." Myriam promises to take control of the situation. Naturally so rigid, so strict, she blames herself for having let things slide. She is going to talk to Louise, get everything out in the open. She is at once embarrassed and secretly thrilled that Louise takes it upon herself to do so much housework, that she accomplishes what she's never been asked to do. Myriam is constantly apologizing. When she gets home late, she says: "I'm sorry for abusing your kindness." And Louise always replies: "That's what I'm here for. Don't worry about it."

Myriam often gives her presents. Earrings that she buys in a discount boutique near the metro station. An orange cake, the only sweet treat that Louise seems to like. She gives the nanny clothes that she doesn't wear anymore, even though for a long time she thought there was something humiliating about that practice. Myriam does everything she can to avoid wounding Louise, to avoid making her jealous or upset. When she goes shopping, for herself or for her children, she hides the new clothes in an old cloth bag and only opens them once Louise has gone. Paul congratulates her on being so tactful.

Everyone in Paul and Myriam's inner circle ends up knowing about Louise. Some of them have seen her in the neighborhood or in the apartment. Others have only heard about the feats of this legendary nanny, who seems to have sprung straight from the pages of a children's book.

"Louise's dinners" become a tradition, an unmissable experience for all the couple's friends. Louise is aware of each person's tastes. She knows that Emma shrewdly conceals her anorexia behind a vegetarian ideology. That Patrick, Paul's brother, is a connoisseur of meat and mushrooms. The dinners generally take place on Friday evenings. Louise spends all afternoon cooking while the children play at her feet. She tidies the apartment, makes a bouquet of flowers and sets the table so it looks pretty. She goes all across Paris to buy a few yards of material, which she uses to hand-stitch a tablecloth. When the places have been set, the sauce reduced and the wine decanted, she slips out of the apartment. Sometimes she bumps into some of the guests in the building's lobby or near the metro station. She replies shyly to their congratulations and their knowing smiles, to the way they pat their stomachs and lick their lips.

One night Paul insists that she stays. This is no ordinary day. "We have so many things to celebrate!" Pascal has given Myriam a very big case, which she is well on her way to winning thanks to an astute, aggressive defense. Paul is also very happy. One week ago, he was in the studio, working on his own music, when a well-known singer came into the producer's booth. They talked for hours, about their shared tastes, the arrangements they imagined for the songs, the incredible material they could get their hands on, and in the end the singer asked Paul to produce his next album. "There are years like that, where everything goes perfectly. You have to know how to enjoy it," Paul declares. He grabs Louise by the shoulders and smiles at her. "Whether you like it or not, tonight you are eating dinner with us."

Louise takes refuge in the children's bedroom. She spends a long time lying next to Mila, caressing her temples and her hair. In the blue glow of the nightlight, she observes Adam's face, surrendered to sleep. She can't make up her mind to leave the room. She hears the front door open and laughter in the corridor. A bottle of champagne is popped open, a chair is pushed against the wall. In the bathroom, Louise reties her bun and puts on some mauve eyeshadow. Myriam never uses makeup. Tonight she is wearing a pair of straight-leg jeans and one of Paul's shirts with the sleeves rolled up.

"I don't think you've met, have you? Pascal, allow me to introduce our Louise. You know everyone is jealous of us for finding her!" Myriam puts her arm around Louise's shoulders. Louise smiles and turns away, slightly embarrassed by the familiarity of the gesture. "Louise, this is Pascal, my boss."

"Your boss? Oh, give me a break! We work together. We're colleagues." Pascal laughs loudly as he shakes Louise's hand.

Louise is sitting at one end of the sofa, her fingers with their long polished nails tensed around her glass of champagne. She is as nervous as a foreigner, an exile who doesn't understand the language being spoken around her. She shares embarrassed, welcoming smiles with the other guests on either side of the coffee table. They lift their glasses to Myriam's talent and to Paul's singer, one of whose melodies someone hums. They talk about their jobs, about terrorism and property prices. Patrick describes his plans for a vacation in Sri Lanka.

Emma, who is sitting next to Louise, talks to her about her children. Louise knows how to talk about that. Emma has worries, which she explains to the reassuring nanny. "I've seen that lots of times, don't worry," Louise repeats. Emma, who has so many anxieties and to whom no one listens, envies Myriam for being able to depend on this Sphinx-like nanny. Emma is a sweet woman, her feelings betrayed only by her constantly wringing hands. She is smiling but envious, a neurotic flirt.

Emma lives in the twentieth arrondissement, in a part of the neighborhood where the squats have been transformed into an organic day care. She lives in a small house, decorated with such taste that it almost makes you uneasy. You have the impression that her living room, crammed with knickknacks and cushions, is designed to provoke envy rather than for its inhabitants' comfort.

"The local school is a disaster. The children spit on the ground. When you walk past it, you hear them calling each other 'whores' and 'queers.' Now, I'm not saying that nobody ever says 'fuck' in their private school. But they say it in a different way, don't you think? At least they know that they're only supposed to say it when no grownups are around. They know it's bad."

Emma has even heard that, at the public school, the one in her street, some parents turn up in pajamas, half an hour late, to drop off their children. That one mother, in a veil, refused to shake hands with the headmaster.

"It's a sad thing to say, but Odin would have been the only white kid in his class. I know we shouldn't give up, but I don't think I'd handle it well if he came back to the house talking about God and speaking Arabic." Myriam smiles at her. "You know what I mean, don't you?"

They stand up, laughing, and move to the table. Paul seats Emma next to him. Louise hurries into the kitchen and she is greeted by bravos when she enters the living room, carrying the meal. "She's blushing," Paul says, amused, in a too-shrill voice. For a few minutes, Louise is the center of attention. "How did she make this sauce?" "Ginger—what a good idea!" The guests vaunt her prowess and Paul starts talking about her—"our nanny"—the way people talk about children and old people in their presence. Paul serves the wine, and the conversations soon rise high above such earthly considerations as food. They speak louder and louder. They stub out their cigarettes in their plates and the butts float in puddles of sauce. No one has noticed that Louise has withdrawn to the kitchen, which she is energetically cleaning.

Myriam shoots an irritated look at Paul. She pretends to laugh at his jokes, but he gets on her nerves when he's drunk. He becomes salacious, tactless, he loses all sense of reality. When he's had too much to drink, he issues invitations to horrible people, makes promises he can't keep. He tells lies. But he doesn't seem to notice his wife's annoyance. He opens another bottle of wine and taps on the edge of the table. "This year, we're going to give ourselves a treat and take our nanny with us on vacation! You have to enjoy life, right?" Louise, a pile of plates in her hands, smiles.

The next morning, Paul wakes up in a crumpled shirt, his lips still stained by red wine. In the shower, fragments of the evening flash up in his memory. He remembers his proposal and the dark look his wife shot him. He feels stupid and tired in advance. He'll have to fix his mistake now. Or pretend he never mentioned it, let time pass, wait for it to be forgotten. He knows that Myriam will make fun of him, of his drunken promises. She will blame him for his financial recklessness and the thoughtless way he treats Louise. "Because of you, she'll be disappointed, but she's so kind, she won't even dare to say anything." Myriam will hold their bills in front of his eyes, bring him back to reality. "It's always like that when you drink," she will conclude.

But Myriam does not seem angry. Lying on the sofa, with Adam in her arms, she smiles at him so sweetly that he can't believe it. She's wearing men's pajamas, too big for her. Paul sits next to her and nuzzles her neck. He loves its heather-like smell. "Is it true what you said last night?" she asks. "You think we can take Louise with us this summer? That'll be so great! For once, we'll have a real vacation. And Louise will be so happy. I mean, what else could she do that'd be better than that?"

It's so hot that Louise has left the window of the hotel room half-open. The shouts of drunkards and the screeching of car brakes do not wake Adam and Mila, who snore, mouths open, one leg dangling out of bed. They are spending only one night in Athens and Louise is sharing a tiny room with the children, to save money. They spent the whole evening laughing. They went to bed late. Adam was happy: he danced in the streets, on the cobblestones of Athens, and old people clapped their hands, captivated by his ballet. Louise did not like the city, which they walked through all afternoon despite the sweltering sun and the whining of the children. She is only thinking about tomorrow, about their trip to the islands, whose myths and legends Myriam has recounted to the children.

Myriam isn't good at telling stories. She has a slightly irritating way of articulating the complicated words and finishes all her sentences with "You see?," "You understand?" But Louise listened, like a studious child, to the story of Zeus and the goddess of war. Like Mila, her favorite was

Aegeus, who gave his blue to the sea, the sea on which she will ride in a boat for the first time.

In the morning, she has to drag Mila out of bed. The little girl is still asleep when the nanny undresses her. In the taxi on the way to the port of Piraeus, Louise tries to remember some ancient gods, but they are all gone from her memory. She should have written the names of those heroes down in her flowered notebook. She would have thought about them again afterward, alone. At the entrance to the port, a huge bottleneck has formed and some policemen are trying to direct traffic. It's already very hot and Adam, sitting on Louise's knees, is soaked with sweat. Massive luminous signs point the way to the docks where the boats for the islands are moored, but Paul doesn't understand them. He gets angry, becomes agitated. The taxi driver makes a U-turn, shrugging with resignation. He doesn't speak English. Paul pays him. They get out of the car and run to their quay, dragging their suitcases and Adam's stroller behind them. The crew are about to raise the bridge when they see the family, frenzied and disheveled, waving their arms about. They were lucky.

No sooner are they on the boat than the children fall asleep, Adam in his mother's arms and Mila with her head resting on Paul's knees. Louise wants to see the sea and the contours of the islands. She goes up on to the bridge. On a bench, a woman is lying on her back. She is wearing a bikini: a thong and a strip of material around her chest that barely hides her breasts. She has very dry platinum-blonde hair, but what strikes Louise is her skin. It is purplish and covered with large brown stains. In places—inside her thighs, on her cheeks, just above her breasts—her skin is blistered and raw, as if she's been burned. She is immobile, like the corpse of a flayed torture victim, left out as a warning to the others.

Louise is seasick. She takes deep breaths. She closes her eyes then opens them, unable to quell the dizziness. She can't move. She sits on a bench, her back to the bridge, far from the edge of the boat. She would like to look at the sea, to remember it, and those white-shored islands that the tourists are pointing at. She would like to memorize the shapes of the sailing boats that have anchored in the sea and the slim figures diving into the water. She would like to, but she feels nauseated.

The sun grows hotter and hotter and now there is a crowd of people staring at the woman on the bench. She has covered her eyes and the sound of the wind probably prevents her from hearing the stifled laughter, the remarks, the whispers. Louise can't stop looking at that scrawny body, streaming with sweat. That woman consumed by the sun, like a piece of meat thrown on the embers.

Paul has rented two bedrooms in a charming guest-house in the island's hills, above a beach where the children spend a lot of time. The sun sets and a pink light envelops the bay. They walk toward Apollonia, the capital. The roads they take are lined with cactuses and fig trees. At the bottom of a cliff is a monastery visited by tourists in swimsuits. Louise is completely entranced by the beauty of the place, by the calmness of the narrow streets, the little squares where cats sleep. She sits on a wall, her feet dangling, and she watches an old woman sweep the courtyard outside her house.

The sun has sunk into the sea, but it isn't dark yet. The light has just taken on shades of pastel and the details of the landscape are still visible. The outline of a bell on the roof of a church. The aquiline profile of a stone bust. The sea and the bushy shore seem to relax, plunged into a languorous torpor, offering themselves to the night, very softly, playing hard to get.

After putting the children to bed, Louise can't sleep. She sits on the terrace outside her room, from where she can contemplate the rounded bay. The wind begins to blow in the evening, a sea wind, in which she can almost taste salt and utopias. She falls asleep there, on a deck-chair, with a shawl covering her like a thin blanket. The cold dawn wakes her and she nearly cries out at the spectacle of the new day. A pure, simple, obvious beauty. A beauty within the reach of every heart.

The children wake too, enthusiastic. The only word on their lips is the sea. Adam wants to roll around in the sand. Mila wants to see fish. As soon as they've finished breakfast, they go down to the beach. Louise wears a loose orange dress, a sort of djellaba that makes Myriam smile. It was Mrs. Rouvier who gave it to her, years before, after telling her: "Oh, you know, I've worn it a lot."

The children are ready. She has smeared them in sun cream and they run straight for the sand. Louise sits with her back to a stone wall. In the shade of a pine tree, knees bent, she watches the sunlight glimmer on the sea. She has never seen anything so beautiful before.

Myriam lies on her front and reads a novel. Paul, who ran four miles before breakfast, is dozing. Louise makes sandcastles. She sculpts an enormous turtle that Adam keeps destroying and she keeps patiently rebuilding. Mila, overwhelmed by the heat, pulls her by the arm. "Come on, Louise, let's go in the sea." The nanny resists. She tells Mila to wait. To sit down with her. "Why don't you help me finish my turtle?" She shows the child some seashells that she's collected and that she places delicately on the shell of her giant turtle.

The pine tree no longer gives enough shade and the heat is growing ever more oppressive. Louise is pouring with sweat and she can no longer think of any argument to oppose the begging child. Mila takes her by the hand and Louise refuses to stand up. She grabs the little girl's wrist and pushes her away so brusquely that Mila falls backward. Louise shouts: "Will you leave me alone?"

Paul opens his eyes. Myriam rushes over to Mila and consoles her weeping daughter. They glare at Louise, furious and disappointed. The nanny retreats, ashamed. They are about to ask her for an explanation when she whispers, slowly: "I didn't tell you this before, but I can't swim."

Paul and Myriam remain silent. They signal Mila, who has started to giggle, to be quiet. Mila mocks her: "Louise is a baby. She doesn't even know how to swim." Paul is embarrassed, and that makes him angry. He blames Louise for having brought her poverty, her frailties all the way here. For having poisoned their day with her martyr's face. He takes the children swimming and Myriam dives back into her book.

The morning is spoiled by Louise's sadness and when they eat lunch on the terrace of a little bar, no one speaks. They have not finished eating when, suddenly, Paul stands up and takes Adam in his arms. He walks to the little shop on the beach. He comes back, hopping, because the sand is burning the soles of his feet. He is holding a packet that he waves in front of Louise and Myriam. "Here you go," he says. The two women do not respond and Louise docilely holds up her arm so Paul can slide an inflatable armband past her elbow. "You're so thin, you can even wear children's armbands!"

All week long, Paul takes Louise swimming. The two of them get up early, and while Myriam and the children stay by the guesthouse swimming pool, Louise and Paul go down to the still-deserted beach. As soon as they reach the wet sand, they hold hands and walk through the water for a long time, toward the horizon. They advance until their feet gently lift up from the sand and their bodies start to float. At that instant, Louise is invariably seized by a feeling of panic that she cannot hide. She cries out and Paul knows that he has to hold her hand even more tightly.

To begin with, he is embarrassed by having to touch Louise's skin. When he teaches her to float on her back, he puts one hand under the back of her neck and the other beneath her bottom. An idiotic thought flashes through his mind and he laughs inwardly: "Louise has a bottom." Louise has a body that trembles under Paul's palms and fingers. A body he had not seen or even suspected before, having considered Louise as part of the world of children or the world of employees. Probably he didn't see her at all. And yet, Louise is not unpleasant to look at. Abandoned to

Paul's hands, the nanny resembles a little doll. A few strands of blonde hair escape from the swimming cap that Myriam bought her. Her light tan has brought out tiny freckles on her cheeks and nose. For the first time, Paul notices the faint blonde down on her face, like the fur on newborn chicks. But there is something prudish and childlike about her, a reserve, that prevents Paul feeling anything as brazen as desire for her.

Louise looks at her feet, which sink into the sand and are licked by the sea. In the boat, Myriam told them that Sifnos owed its past prosperity to the gold and silver mines under its earth. And Louise convinces herself that the sparkles she can see through the water, on the rocks, are shards of those precious metals. The cool water covers her thighs. Now her sex organs are submerged. The sea is calm, translucent. Not a single wave surprises Louise or splashes against her chest. There are babies sitting close to the edge of the sea, watched serenely by their parents. When the water reaches her waist, Louise can't breathe anymore. She looks at the sky, dazzling, unreal. She pats the yellow-and-blue armbands on her thin arms, with drawings of a lobster and a triton-snail shell on them. She stares at Paul, imploringly. "There's no risk," Paul promises. "As long as you can stand up, there's no risk at all." But Louise seems petrified. She feels she's about to tip over. That she's going to be snatched by the currents below, her head held underwater, her legs kicking at air, until she can't struggle anymore.

She remembers how, when she was a child, one of her classmates fell in a pond during the village outing. It was a small expanse of muddy water, with a smell in the summer that sickened her. The children went there to play, despite their parents' warnings, despite the mosquitoes drawn there by the stagnant water. Here, in the blue of the Aegean Sea, Louise thinks about that black, stinking water, and about the child found with his face buried in the mire. Ahead of her, Mila kicks her legs. She is floating.

They're drunk and they are climbing the stone stairs that lead to the terrace next to the children's bedroom. They laugh and Louise sometimes clings to Paul's arm to climb up a step that is higher than the others. She gets her breath back, sitting under the bright-red bougainvillea, and looks down below at the beach where young couples drink cocktails and dance. The bar has organized a party on the beach. A "Full Moon Party" for the round, red rock that has shone down on them all evening, with all the guests commenting on its beauty. Louise had never seen a moon like that before, a moon so beautiful it was worth lassoing. Not a cold, gray moon, like the moons of her childhood.

On the terrace of the restaurant in the hills, they contemplated the bay of Sifnos and the lava-colored sunset. Paul pointed out the lacy clouds. The tourists took photographs and when Louise wanted to stand up too to get a snapshot of it with her mobile phone, Paul gently pulled her arm to make her sit down again. "It won't capture it. Better just to remember what it looks like."

For the first time, the three of them eat dinner together. The guesthouse owner offered to look after the children. They are the same age as his and they have been inseparable since the start of the vacation. Myriam and Paul were caught unprepared. Louise, of course, began by refusing. She said she couldn't leave them alone, that she had to put them to bed. That it was her job. "They've been swimming all day, they won't have any trouble falling asleep," the owner said in bad French.

So they walked to the restaurant, in a slightly awkward silence. At the table, they all drank more than usual. Myriam and Paul were dreading this dinner. What could they talk about? What would they have to say to one another? But they were convinced that it was the right thing to do, that Louise would be content. "I want her to know that we value her work, you understand?" So they talk about the children, the landscape, the morning swim, Mila's progress with the breaststroke. They make conversation. Louise wants to tell them something—doesn't matter what, something about her—but she doesn't dare. She inhales deeply, moves her face forward to say something then draws back, tongue-tied. They drink and the silence grows peaceful, languorous.

Paul, who is sitting next to her, puts his arm around her shoulders. The ouzo has made him jovial. He squeezes her shoulder with his big hand, smiles at her like she's an old friend, like they're friends forever. She stares, enchanted, at the man's face. His tanned skin, his large white teeth, his hair turned blond by the wind and the salt. He shakes her a little bit, the way you do with a friend who's shy or sad, with someone you want to relax or get a grip.

If she dared, she'd put her hand on Paul's hand, she'd grip it with her slender fingers. But she doesn't dare.

She is fascinated by Paul's easy assurance. He jokes around with the waiter, who brings them each a *digestif*. In a few days he has already learned enough Greek to make the shopkeepers laugh or give him a discount. People recognize him. On the beach, he's the one that the other children want to play with. Laughing, he bows to their desires. He carries them on his back, he jumps in the water with them. He eats with an incredible appetite. Myriam seems irritated by this, but Louise is touched by his love of food, which drives him to order everything on the menu. "We'll take that too. We have to try it, right?" And he picks up the pieces of meat or pepper or cheese with his fingers and swallows them with innocent joy.

Back on the guesthouse terrace, the three of them burst out laughing into their hands and Louise puts a finger to her lips. Mustn't wake the little ones. This flash of responsibility suddenly strikes them as ludicrous. They play at being children, these adults whose whole day has been spent straining toward the same child-centered objective. Tonight a new lightheartedness blows over them. Their intoxication relieves the accumulated anxieties and tensions that their progeny has insinuated between them, husband and wife, mother and nanny.

Louise knows how fleeting this moment is. She sees Paul staring greedily at his wife's shoulder. Against her pale-blue dress, Myriam's skin appears even more golden. They start to dance, swaying from side to side. They are clumsy, almost embarrassed, and Myriam giggles as if it's been a long time since anyone held her around the waist like this. As if she felt ridiculous to be desired in this way. Myriam puts her cheek on her husband's shoulder. Louise knows that they are going to stop, say good-bye, pretend to be sleepy. She would like to hold them back, to cling to them, scratch her nails in the stone floor. She would like to put them under glass, like two dancers, frozen and smiling, stuck to the pedestal of a musical box. She thinks that she could stare at them for hours without ever getting bored. That she would be content to watch them live, working in the shadows so that everything was perfect, so that the mechanism never jammed. She has the intimate conviction now, the burning and painful conviction that her happiness belongs to them. That she is theirs and they are hers.

Paul giggles. He whispers something, his lips deep in his wife's neck. Something that Louise doesn't hear. He keeps a firm hold of Myriam's hand and, like two polite children, they wish Louise good night. She watches them climb the stone staircase that leads to their bedroom. The blue line of their two bodies blurs, fades, the door slams shut. The curtains are drawn. Louise sinks into an obscene daydream. She hears, without wanting to, while refusing to, despite herself. She hears Myriam's wailing, her doll-like moans. She hears the rustle of sheets and the headboard banging against the wall.

Louise opens her eyes. Adam is crying.

ROSE GRINBERG

Mrs. Grinberg will describe this little journey in the elevator at least a hundred times. Five stories, after a brief wait on the ground floor. A journey of less than two minutes, which has become the most poignant moment of her life. The fateful moment. She could—as she will never cease repeating—have altered the course of events. If she'd paid more attention to Louise's breath. If she hadn't closed her windows and shutters to take her nap. She will cry over the telephone and her daughters will not be able to reassure her. The police will become irritated that she is giving so much importance to herself and her tears will fall more heavily when she tells them coldly: "Well, *you* couldn't have done anything, anyway." She will tell everything to the journalists who are following the trial. She will speak about it to the defendant's lawyer, whom she will find arrogant and sloppy, and repeat it in the courtroom, when she is summoned to testify.

Louise, she will say each time, was not her normal self. Usually so smiling and friendly, she stood motionless in front of the glass door. Adam, sitting on a step, was screaming loudly and Mila was jumping, knocking into her brother. Louise did not move. Only her lower lip trembled slightly. Her hands were joined and her eyes lowered. For once, the noise of the children did not seem to affect her. Though normally so concerned for the neighbors and keeping up appearances, she did not say a word to the little ones. It was as if she couldn't hear them.

Mrs. Grinberg liked Louise a lot. She could even say she admired this elegant woman who took such good care of the children. Mila, the little girl, always had her hair tied in tight braids or a bun held in place by a knot. Adam seemed to adore Louise. "Now she's done what she did, maybe I shouldn't say this. But at that moment I thought they were lucky."

The bell rang and the ground-floor light came on. Louise grabbed Adam by the collar and dragged him into the elevator. Mila followed, singing to herself. Mrs. Grinberg hesitated before getting in with them. For a few seconds she wondered if she should go back into the lobby and pretend to check her letterbox. Louise's pale face made her uneasy. She feared that the five-story journey would feel interminable. But Louise was holding the door for the neighbor, who got in and stood against the wall of the elevator, her shopping bag between her legs.

"Did she appear drunk?"

Mrs. Grinberg had no doubt. Louise appeared completely sober. She couldn't have let her go up with the children if she'd thought for a second that . . . The gray-haired female lawyer mocked her. She reminded the court that Rose suffered from dizzy spells and had vision problems. The former music teacher, who would soon celebrate her sixty-fifth birthday, couldn't see very well anymore. Not only that, but she lived in the dark, like a mole. Bright light gave her terrible migraines. That was why Rose closed the shutters. That was why she didn't hear anything.

That lawyer practically insulted her, in front of the whole court. Rose desperately wanted to shut her up, to break her jaw. Wasn't she ashamed? Didn't she have any decency? From the first days of the trial, the lawyer had portrayed Myriam as an "absent mother," an "abusive employer." She'd described her as a woman blinded by ambition, selfish and indifferent to the point where she pushed poor Louise too far. A journalist seated near Mrs. Grinberg in the courtroom explained to her that there was no point getting upset; that it was merely a "defense tactic." But Rose thought it was disgusting, full stop.

No one talks about it in the apartment building but Mrs. Grinberg knows that everyone is thinking it. That at night, on every floor, eyes remain open in the darkness. That hearts race, and tears fall. She knows that bodies toss and turn, unable to fall asleep. The couple on the third floor have moved away. The Massés, of course, never came back. Rose has stayed despite the ghosts and the overpowering memory of that scream.

That day, after her nap, she opened the shutters. And that was when she heard it. Most people live their whole lives without ever hearing a scream like that. It is the kind of scream heard during war, in the trenches, in other worlds, on other continents. It is not a scream from here. It lasted at least ten minutes, that wordless scream, almost without a pause for breath. That scream that became hoarse, that filled with blood, with snot, with rage. "A doctor" was all that Mrs. Massé ended up articulating. She didn't cry for help, she merely repeated—in the rare moments when she flickered back into consciousness—"A doctor."

One month before the tragedy, Mrs. Grinberg had met Louise in the street. The nanny had looked worried and in the end she'd talked about her money problems. About her landlord who was harassing her, about the debts she'd accumulated, about her bank account, constantly in the red. She'd talked the way a balloon deflates, more and more quickly.

Mrs. Grinberg had pretended not to understand. She'd lowered her chin and said, "Times are hard for everyone." And then Louise had grabbed her by the arm. "I'm not begging. I can work, in the evening or early in the morning. When the children are asleep. I can clean the apartment, iron clothes, whatever you want." If she hadn't gripped her wrist so tightly, if she hadn't stared at her with those dark eyes, like an insult or a threat, Rose Grinberg might have accepted. And, no matter what the police say, she would have changed everything.

The flight was delayed for a long time and it is early evening when they land in Paris. Louise solemnly says goodbye to the children. She hugs them tight and doesn't let go. "See you on Monday, yes, Monday. Call me if you need anything at all," she says to Myriam and Paul, who dive into the elevator that will take them to the airport parking lot.

Louise walks to the overground train station. The carriage is empty. She sits leaning against a window and curses the landscape, the platforms where gangs of youths hang around, the peeling facades of apartment buildings, the balconies, the hostile faces of security guards. She closes her eyes and summons memories of Greek beaches, sunsets, dinners overlooking the sea. She invokes these memories the way mystics call upon miracles. When she opens the door to her studio flat, her hands start to shake. She wants to tear apart the sofa's slipcover, to punch the window. A sort of shapeless, painful magma burns her insides and it takes an effort of will to stop herself screaming.

On Saturday she stays in bed until 10 a.m. Lying on

the sofa, hands crossed over her chest, Louise looks at the dust that has accumulated on the green ceiling lamp. She would never have chosen something so ugly. She rented the apartment already furnished and has not changed any of the decor. She had to find somewhere to live after the death of her husband, Jacques, after her expulsion from the house. After weeks of wandering, she needed a nest. She found this studio, in Créteil, through a nurse in the Henri-Mondor hospital who became fond of her. The young woman assured her that the landlord wouldn't ask for too much in the way of security and that he'd accept cash payments.

Louise stands up. She pushes a chair underneath the ceiling lamp and grabs a cloth. She starts scrubbing the lamp, holding it with such force that she almost rips it off the ceiling. She is on tiptoes and the dust falls in big gray flakes into her hair. By eleven, the whole apartment has been cleaned. She's washed the windows, inside and out, and she's even wiped the shutters with a soapy sponge. Her shoes are lined up along the wall, polished and ridiculous.

Perhaps they will call her. On Saturdays, she knows, they sometimes eat lunch at a restaurant. Mila told her that. They go to a café where the little girl is allowed to order anything she wants and where Adam tries tasting a bit of mustard or lemon from the end of a spoon, under his parents' tender gaze. Louise would like that. In a packed café, surrounded by the din of clanking plates and waiters' shouts, she would be less afraid of the silence. She would sit between Mila and her brother and she'd straighten the large white napkin on the little girl's lap. She'd feed Adam, spoon after spoon. She'd listen to Paul and Myriam speak. It would all go too fast. She would feel good.

She puts on a blue dress, the one that comes down to her ankles and that buttons, up the front, with a row of little blue pearls. She wants to be ready, in case they need her. In case she has to meet them somewhere, quickly, because they've undoubtedly forgotten how far away she lives and how long it takes her, every day, to get to their apartment. Sitting in the kitchen, she drums the Formica table with her fingernails.

Lunchtime comes and goes. The clouds move in front of the clean windows, the sky darkens. The plane trees shake in the wind and it starts to rain. Louise becomes agitated. They're not going to call.

It is too late now to leave the apartment. She could go and buy some bread or get some fresh air. She could just walk. But there is nothing she wants to do in these deserted streets. The only café in the neighborhood is full of drunks, and even at three in the afternoon men sometimes brawl there near the railings of the empty garden.

She should have made her mind up earlier, rushed down into the metro, wandered around Paris, surrounded by parents buying school supplies. She'd have got lost in the crowd and she'd have followed beautiful, busy women as they walked past department stores. She'd have hung around near Madeleine, brushing past the little tables where people drink coffee. She'd have said "Sorry" to the ones she bumped into.

Paris is, in her eyes, a giant shop window. Best of all, she likes to walk in the Opéra neighborhood, going down Rue Royale and turning on to Rue Saint-Honoré. She walks slowly, observing the passersby and the shopfronts. She wants everything. The buckskin boots, the suede jackets, the snakeskin handbags, the wrap dresses, the camisoles overstitched with lace. She wants the silk blouses, the pink cashmere cardigans, the military jackets. She imagines a life where she would have enough money to possess it all. Where she would point out to an unctuous saleswoman the items that she liked.

Sunday arrives, an extension of her boredom and anxiety. A dark, miserable Sunday sunk deep in her sofa bed. She fell asleep in her blue dress and its synthetic material, horribly creased, made her sweat. Several times during the night, she opened her eyes, unsure if an hour had passed or a month. If she was sleeping at Myriam and Paul's apartment or next to Jacques in the house in Bobigny. Then she closed her eyes again and slid back into a brutal, frenzied sleep.

Louise really hates weekends. When they still lived together, Stéphanie used to complain that they never did anything on Sundays, that she wasn't allowed any of the activities Louise organized for the other children. As soon as she could, she started fleeing the house. On Fridays she would be out all night with the neighborhood teenagers. She'd come back in the morning, face pale, eyes red with rings around them. Starving. She'd walk across the small living room, head lowered, and aim straight for the fridge. She would eat, leaning against the fridge door, without even sitting down, digging with her fingers into the boxes that Louise had prepared for Jacques's lunches. Once, she dyed her hair red. She had her nose pierced. She started disappearing for entire weekends. And then, one day, she didn't come back. Nothing now could keep her at the house in Bobigny. Not school, which she'd left a long time ago. And not Louise either.

Her mother reported her disappearance, of course. "Kids that age, running away, it happens a lot. Wait a bit and she'll be back." That was all they said to her. Louise didn't search for her. Later she found out from neighbors that Stéphanie was in the South of France, that she was in love. That she moved around a lot. The neighbors couldn't get over the fact that Louise didn't ask them for details, didn't ask any questions, didn't want them to repeat the little information they had.

Stéphanie had disappeared. All her life, she had felt like an embarrassment. Her presence disturbed Jacques, her laughter woke the children Louise was looking after. Her fat thighs, her heavy figure pressed against the wall in the narrow corridor to let the others pass. She feared blocking the passage, being bumped into, sitting on a chair that someone else wanted. When she spoke, she expressed herself poorly. She laughed and she offended people, no matter how innocent her laughter. She had ended up developing a gift for invisibility, and logically, without fanfare, without warning, as if that had been her manifest destiny all along, she had disappeared.

On Monday morning Louise leaves her apartment before daybreak. She walks to the train station, changes at Auber, waits on the platform, walks up Rue Lafayette then takes Rue d'Hauteville. Louise is a soldier. She keeps going, come what may, like a mule, like a dog with its legs broken by cruel children.

September is hot and bright. On Wednesdays, after school, Louise shakes up the children's stay-at-home indolence and takes them to play in the park or to watch the fish in the aquarium. They go boating on the lake in the Bois de Boulogne and Louise tells Mila that the algae floating on the surface is in reality the hair of a deposed, vengeance-seeking witch. At the end of the month it is so warm that Louise, excited, decides to take them to the botanical gardens.

Outside the metro station, an old North African man offers to help Louise carry the stroller down the stairs. She thanks him and picks up the stroller single-handed with Adam still sitting inside it. The old man follows her. He asks how old the children are. She is about to tell him that they are not hers. But he is already leaning down to the children's level. "They're very beautiful."

The metro is the children's favorite thing. If Louise didn't hold them back, they'd run along the platform, they'd jump into the carriage, standing on people's feet, just so they could sit next to the window, tongues lolling, eyes wide open. They stand inside the carriage and Adam imitates his sister, who is holding on to a metal bar and pretending to drive the train.

In the gardens, the nanny runs with them. They laugh and she spoils them, buying them ice creams and balloons. She takes a picture of them, lying on a carpet of dead leaves, bright yellow and blood red. Mila asks why certain trees have turned that luminous shade of gold while others, the same kinds of trees, planted next to them, look like they're rotting, going straight from green to dark brown. Louise is incapable of explaining. "We'll ask your mama," she says.

On the fairground rides, they howl with terror and joy. Louise feels dizzy and she holds Adam tight in her lap when the train rushes into the dark tunnels and hurtles down the slopes. In the sky, a balloon flies away: Mickey has become a spaceship.

They sit on the grass to picnic and Mila makes fun of Louise, who is afraid of the large peacocks a few yards from them. The nanny has brought an old wool blanket that Myriam had rolled up in a ball under her bed and that Louise cleaned and mended. The three of them fall asleep on the grass. Louise wakes up, with Adam pressed against her. She's cold: the children must have pulled the blanket off. She turns around and doesn't see Mila. She calls her. She starts to scream. People turn to stare. Someone asks: "Is everything all right, madam? Do you need help?" She doesn't answer. "Mila, Mila," she screams as she runs, with Adam in her arms. She goes around all the rides, runs in front of the rifle range. Tears well in her eyes. She wants to shake the passersby, to push the strangers who are hurrying along, holding their children firmly by their hands. She turns back to the little farmhouse. Her jaw is trembling so much that she can't even call Mila's name anymore. Her head is killing her and she feels as if her knees are about to give way. In an instant, she will fall to the ground, incapable of making the slightest movement, mute, completely helpless.

Then she spots her, at the end of a path. Mila is eating an ice cream on a bench, a woman leaning toward her. Louise throws herself at the child. "Mila! Have you gone mad? Why on earth did you go away like that?"

The stranger—a woman in her sixties—holds the little girl protectively. "It's a disgrace. What were you doing? How could she end up alone? I could easily ask this little girl for her parents' number. I'm not sure they would be too happy about it."

But Mila escapes the stranger's embrace. She pushes her away and glares at her, before throwing herself at Louise's legs. The nanny bends down and picks her up. Louise kisses her frozen neck, she strokes her hair. She looks at the child's pale face and apologizes for her negligence. "My little one, my angel, my sweet." She cuddles her, covers her with kisses, holds her tight against her chest.

Seeing the child curled up in the arms of the little blonde woman, the old lady calms down. She no longer knows what to say. She observes them, shaking her head reproachfully. She was probably hoping to cause a scandal. That would have distracted her. She'd have had something to tell people if the nanny had got angry, if she'd had to call the parents, if threats had been made and then carried out. Finally the stranger gets up from the bench and leaves, saying: "Well, next time, be more careful."

Louise watches the old lady leave. She turns around two or three times and Louise smiles at her, grateful. As her stooped figure moves away, Louise holds Mila more and more strongly against her. She crushes the little girl's torso until she begs: "Stop, Louise, I can't breathe." The child tries to free herself from this embrace—she wriggles and kicks—but the nanny holds her firmly in place. She sticks her lips to Mila's ear and says to her, in a cold, composed voice: "Never do that again, you hear me? Do you want someone to kidnap you? A nasty man? Next time, that's what will happen. And even if you shout and cry, no one will come. Do you know what he'll do to you? No? You don't know? He'll take you away, he'll hide you, he'll keep you for himself and you'll never see your parents again." Louise is about to put the child down when she feels a terrible pain in her shoulder. She screams and tries to shove the little girl away from her. Mila is biting her. Her teeth are sunk in Louise's flesh, tearing it, drawing blood, and she clings to Louise's arm like a rabid animal.

That night, she doesn't tell Myriam about her daughter running away, nor about the bite. Mila, too, remains silent, without the nanny warning or threatening her. Now Louise and Mila each have a grievance against the other. This secret unites them as never before.

JACQUES

Jacques loved telling her to shut up. He couldn't stand her voice, which grated on his nerves. "Shut it, will you?" In the car, she couldn't help chatting. She was frightened of the road and talking calmed her. She launched into insipid monologues, barely taking a breath between sentences. She jabbered away blandly, listing names of streets, rolling out old memories.

She felt good when her husband yelled at her. She knew that it was to shut her up that he turned up the volume on the radio. That it was to humiliate her that he opened the window and began to smoke, while humming. Her spouse's anger scared her, but she had to admit that, sometimes, it excited her too. She enjoyed making him writhe, working him up into such a state of rage that he was capable of parking on the roadside, grabbing her by the throat and quietly threatening that he would shut her up for good.

Jacques was heavy, noisy. As he got older, he became bitter and vain. In the evenings, coming home from work, he would rant on for at least an hour about his grievances with this or that person. According to him, everyone was trying to steal from him, manipulate him, take advantage of his condition. After his first redundancy, he took his employer to an industrial tribunal. The trial cost him time and a huge amount of money, but his final victory gave him a feeling of such power that he got a taste for disputes and courtrooms. Later he thought he could make his fortune by suing his insurance company after a car accident. Next he went after the first-floor neighbors, the town hall, the building's management company. Whole days were spent writing illegible, threatening letters. He would go through legal-aid websites in search of any article of law that might play in his favor. Jacques was irascible and utterly hypocritical. He envied the success of others, denying them any merit. Sometimes he would even spend all afternoon at the commercial court, just to binge on others' sufferings. He enjoyed seeing people ruined, the blows of fate.

"I'm not like you," he told Louise proudly. "I'm not a doormat, a slave content to clean up the shit and puke of little brats. Only black women do work like that now." He thought his wife excessively docile. And while that excited him at night, in their conjugal bed, it exasperated him the rest of the time. He was forever giving Louise advice, which she pretended to listen to. "You should tell them to reimburse you, and that's it"; "You shouldn't agree to work one minute more without being paid"; "Just call in sick— what do you think they can do about it?"

Jacques was too busy to look for a job. His legal battles took up all his time. He hardly set foot outside the apartment, spreading his case files over the coffee table and leaving the television on. During that period, the presence of children became unbearable to him and he ordered Louise to work in her employers' apartment. He was irritated by the sound of their coughs and wails, even their laughter. Louise, most of all, revolted him. Her pathetic preoccupations, which always centered on kids, put him in a veritable rage. "You and your bloody women's things," he would repeat. He believed that such matters should not be talked about. Just let them get on with it, somewhere out of sight; we don't need to know anything about all this stuff with babies or old people. They were bad times, those ages of servitude, of repeating the same actions. Those ages when the body—monstrous, shameless, a cold and foul-smelling machine—took over everything. Bodies that craved love and liquid. "It's enough to make you disgusted at being a man."

During that period, he bought—on credit—a computer, a new television and an electrically powered chair that gave massages and that could be inclined when he wanted to take a nap. He would spend hours in front of the computer's blue screen, his asthmatic wheezes filling the room. Sitting on his new chair, facing his brand-new television, he would frantically press the buttons on his remote control, like an overexcited kid.

It was probably a Saturday, since they ate lunch together. Jacques was ranting, as always, but with less vigor than usual. Under the table, Louise had put a bowl of ice water in which Jacques was soaking his feet. In her nightmares, Louise can still see Jacques's purple legs, his swollen diabetic's ankles, which he would constantly ask her to massage. For the past few days, Louise had noticed, his complexion had been waxy, his eyes dull. He'd been having difficulty finishing a sentence without pausing for breath. She cooked an osso buco. After his third mouthful, as he was about to speak, Jacques threw it up all over his plate. It was projectile vomit, like a baby's, and Louise knew it must be serious. That he wouldn't get better. She stood up and, seeing Jacques's bewildered expression, she said: "Don't worry, it's nothing." She talked constantly, accusing herself of having put too much wine in the sauce, which had made it acidic, spouting idiotic theories about heartburn. She talked and talked, gave advice, blamed herself and asked for forgiveness. Her quavering, incoherent logorrhea only succeeded in intensifying the panic that had taken hold of Jacques, a fear akin to missing the top step of a staircase and seeing himself tumbling down, headfirst, his spine crushed, his flesh bloody. If she'd shut up, perhaps he could have wept, maybe he'd have asked for help or even a bit of tenderness. But as she cleared the table, as she cleaned the floor, she talked, ceaselessly.

Jacques died three months later. He dried up like a piece of fruit forgotten in the sun. It was snowing on the day of his funeral and the light was almost blue. Louise found herself alone.

She nodded as the notary explained, in an apologetic voice, that Jacques had left her only debts. She stared at the goiter crushed under his shirt collar and pretended to accept the situation. All she had inherited from Jacques were failed lawsuits, pending trials, unpaid bills. The bank gave her a month to leave the little house in Bobigny, which would be repossessed. Louise boxed everything up herself. She carefully collected the few things that Stéphanie had left behind. She didn't know what to do with the piles of documents that Jacques had accumulated. She thought about setting fire to them in the little garden, imagining that, with a bit of luck, the blaze might spread to the house, the street, even the whole neighborhood. In that way, this entire part of her life would go up in smoke. She would feel no sorrow if it did. She would stay there, motionless, discreet, to watch the flames devour her memories, her long walks in the dark empty streets, her bored Sundays with Jacques and Stéphanie.

But Louise picked up her suitcase, she double-locked the door and she left, abandoning in the entrance hall of the little house those boxes of memories, her daughter's clothes and her husband's schemes.

That night she slept in a hotel room, where she paid for a week's stay in advance. She made sandwiches and ate them in front of the television. She sucked fig biscuits, letting them melt on her tongue. Solitude was like a vast hole into which Louise watched herself sink. Solitude, which stuck to her flesh, to her clothes, began to model her features, making her move like a little old lady. Solitude leaped at her face at dusk, when night fell and the sounds of family lives rose from the surrounding houses. The light dimmed and the murmur grew louder: laughter, panting, even sighs of boredom.

In that room, on a street in the Chinese quarter, she lost all notion of time. She felt lost, crazed. The whole world had forgotten her. She would sleep for hours and wake up swollen-eyed, her head aching, despite the cold that seethed through the room. She only went out when she absolutely had to, when her hunger became too painful to ignore. She walked in the street as if it were a cinema set and she were not there, an invisible spectator to the movements of mankind. Everyone seemed to have somewhere to go.

Solitude was like a drug that she wasn't sure she wanted to do without. Louise wandered through the streets in a daze, eyes so wide open that they hurt. In her solitude, she started to see other people. To really see them. The existence of others became palpable, vibrant, more real than ever. She observed, in minute detail, the gestures of couples sitting on terraces. The sideways glances of torpid old people. The self-conscious expressions of students who sat on benches and pretended to revise. In squares, outside metro stations, she would recognize the strange parade of the impatient. Like them, she waited for someone. Every day, she would encounter companions in madness: tramps, lunatics, talking to themselves.

The city, back then, was full of madmen.

Winter comes, and the days blur into each other. November is rainy and cold. Outside, the sidewalks are covered with black ice. Impossible to go out. Louise tries to entertain the children. She invents games, she sings songs. They build a house out of cardboard. But the day seems to last forever. Adam has a fever and he won't stop whining. Louise holds him in her arms; she rocks him for nearly an hour, until he falls asleep. Mila, pacing around the living room, grows fractious too.

"Come here," Louise tells her. Mila approaches and the nanny takes from her handbag the little white vanity case that the child has so often daydreamed about. Mila thinks Louise is the most beautiful woman she knows. She looks like the flight attendant—blonde, with lots of makeup—who gave her candies on a trip to Nice. Even though Louise is constantly on the move, doing the washing-up and running from the school to the house, she always looks perfect. Her hair is meticulously tied back. Her black mascara, of which she applies at least three thick coats, makes her look like a surprised doll. And then there are her hands, which are soft and smell of flowers. And her nail polish that never flakes or peels.

Sometimes Louise paints her nails in front of Mila and the little girl, eyes closed, breathes in the smell of the remover and the cheap polish that the nanny spreads with quick, lively gestures, never getting any on her skin. Fascinated, the child watches Louise wave her hands in the air and blow on the fingers.

When Mila allows Louise to kiss her, it is so she can smell the talcum powder on her cheeks, so she can get a closer look at the glitter that sparkles on her eyelids. She likes to watch her put lipstick on. With one hand, Louise holds a mirror—always perfectly clean—in front of her, while she pulls her face into a strange grimace that Mila tries to reproduce afterward in the bathroom.

Louise rummages around in her vanity case. She holds the little girl's hands and coats them with rose-scented cream, which she takes from a tiny pot. "Smells nice, doesn't it?" Under the child's astonished eyes, Louise puts polish on her little nails. A vulgar pink polish that smells very strongly of acetone. For Mila, this is the smell of femininity.

"Take off your socks, would you?" And she paints the toenails of her chubby little feet with nail polish. Louise empties out the contents of the vanity case on the table. The air fills with orange dust and the smell of talc. Mila laughs suddenly, jubilantly. Louise is putting lipstick on her now, then blue eyeshadow, then a sort of orange paste on her cheeks. She asks her to lower her head and she backcombs her hair—too straight and too fine—until it looks like a mane.

They laugh so hard that they don't hear Paul as he closes the front door behind him and enters the living room. Mila smiles, mouth open, arms spread wide.

"Look, Papa. Look what Louise did!"

Paul stares at her. He had been so pleased to get home early, so happy to see his children, but now he feels sick. He has the feeling that he has walked in on something sordid or abnormal. His daughter, his little girl, looks like a transvestite, like a ruined old drag queen. He can't believe it. He is furious, out of control. He hates Louise for having done this. Mila, his angel, his little blue dragonfly, is as ugly as a circus freak, as ridiculous as a dog dressed up for a walk by its hysterical old-lady owner.

"What the hell is this? What did you do to her?" Paul yells. He grabs Mila by the arms and stands her on a stool in the bathroom. He tries to wipe the makeup off her face. The little girl cries out: "You're hurting me." She sobs and the rouge just smears, ever thicker, ever stickier, over the child's diaphanous skin. He has the impression that he is disfiguring her even more, soiling her, and his rage grows.

"Louise, I'm warning you: I never want to see this again. This kind of thing disgusts me. I have no intention of teaching such vulgar behavior to my daughter. She's far too young to dress up like a . . . You know what I mean."

Louise stands in the bathroom doorway, holding Adam in her arms. Despite his father's anger, despite the agitation, the baby doesn't cry. He glares at Paul coldly, suspiciously, as if to make it clear that he is on Louise's side. The nanny listens to Paul. She does not lower her eyes or apologize.

Stéphanie could be dead. Louise thinks about this sometimes. She could have prevented her from ever living. No one would have known. No one would have blamed her. If Louise had eliminated her, society would perhaps even have been grateful to her today. She would have proved herself clear-headed, a good citizen.

Louise was twenty-five years old and she woke up one morning with heavy, painful breasts. A new sadness had come between her and the world. She felt certain that there was something wrong. Back then, she was working for Mr. Franck, an artist who lived with his mother in a mansion in the fourteenth arrondissement. Louise did not really understand Mr. Franck's paintings. In the living room, on the walls of the corridor and the bedrooms, she would stand in front of the immense portraits of disfigured women—bodies crippled with pain or paralyzed in ecstasy—that had made the artist famous. Louise wasn't sure they were beautiful, but she liked them.

Geneviève, Mr. Franck's mother, had fractured the

neck of her femur getting down from a train. Unable to walk, she had lost her mind on the platform. She spent her life lying down—naked, most of the time—in a light-filled ground-floor bedroom. It was so difficult to dress her—she fought with such ferocity—that they just laid her on an open diaper, her breasts and genitals exposed. The sight of that abandoned body was appalling.

Mr. Franck had begun by hiring qualified, very expensive nurses. But they complained about the old woman's tantrums. They stuffed her full of tranquilizers. The son found these nurses cold and brutal. What he wanted for his mother was a friend, a nanny, a tender-hearted woman who would listen to her ravings without rolling her eyes, without sighing. Louise was young, admittedly, but she had impressed him with her physical strength. On the first day, she had come into the bedroom and, by herself, had managed to lift that body, as heavy as a concrete slab. She had cleaned the old woman, talking constantly, and for once Geneviève had not screamed.

Louise slept with Geneviève. She washed her. She listened to her rant all night. Like a baby, the old woman dreaded dusk. The fading light, the shadows, the silences made her scream with fear. She begged her own mother—who'd been dead for forty years—to come and fetch her. Louise, who slept next to the medical bed, tried to calm her down. The old woman spat insults at her, called her a whore, a bitch, a peasant. Sometimes she would try to hit her.

Louise started sleeping more deeply than ever. Geneviève's cries didn't disturb her anymore. Soon she was no longer capable of turning the old woman over or putting her in her wheelchair. It was as if her arms had atrophied, and she had terrible backache. One afternoon, when darkness had already fallen and Geneviève was mumbling heartrending prayers, Louise went up to Mr. Franck's attic to explain the situation to him. To Louise's surprise, the artist became enraged. He banged the door shut and walked over to her, his gray eyes boring into hers. For an instant, she thought he was going to hurt her. And he started laughing.

"Louise, women like you—single women who hardly earn enough money to live—do not have children. To be perfectly honest with you, I think you're completely irresponsible. You turn up here with your big round eyes and your stupid smile, to tell me that. What do you expect me to do? Open a bottle of champagne?" He was pacing around the large room, hands behind his back, surrounded by unfinished paintings. "You think it's good news? Don't you have any common sense at all? I'll tell you one thing: you're lucky you have an employer like me, who's willing to try to help you improve your situation. I know plenty who would kick you out the door, quick as a flash. Listen, I entrust you with my mother, who is the most important person in the world for me, and I can tell that you're completely brainless, incapable of making a good decision. I couldn't care less what you do with your free evenings. Your light morals are none of my business. But life is not a party. What would you do with a baby?"

In reality, Mr. Franck did care what Louise did with her Saturday evenings. He started asking her questions, increasingly insistent. He wanted to shake her, to slap her face until she confessed. He wanted her to tell him what she did when she wasn't there, at Geneviève's bedside, where he could keep an eye on her. He wanted to know from what caresses this child had been conceived, in which bed Louise had abandoned herself to pleasure, to lust, to laughter. He asked her over and over again who the father was, what he looked like, where she'd met him and what his intentions were. But Louise, invariably, responded to his questions by saying: "He's no one."

Mr. Franck took charge of everything. He said he would drive Louise to the doctor himself and wait for her during the procedure. He even promised her that once it was over, he would have her sign a proper contract, that he would pay money into a bank account in her name, and that she would have the right to paid vacations.

The day of the operation, Louise overslept and missed the appointment. Stéphanie took over her life, digging inside her, stretching her, tearing apart her youth. She grew like a mushroom on a damp piece of wood. Louise did not go back to Mr. Franck's house. She never saw the old lady again.

Locked up in the Massés' apartment, she sometimes feels she is going mad. For the past few days there have been red blotches on her cheeks and her wrists. Louise has to put her hands and her face under cold water to soothe the burning sensation. During the long winter days, a feeling of immense solitude grips her. In a panic, she leaves the apartment, closes the door behind her, faces up to the cold and takes the children to the park.

Parks, on winter afternoons. The drizzle scatters dead leaves. The icy gravel sticks to the children's knees. On benches, on narrow paths, you see those people the world doesn't want anymore. They flee cramped apartments, sad living rooms, armchairs sunk with the imprint of boredom and inertia. They prefer to shiver outside, shoulders hunched and arms crossed. At 4 p.m., idle days seem endless. It is now, in the middle of the afternoon, that you notice the wasted time, that you worry about the coming evening. At this hour, you are ashamed of your uselessness.

Parks, on winter afternoons, are haunted by vaga-bonds, drifters, tramps, the elderly and unemployed, the sick, the vulnerable. Those who do not work, who produce nothing. Those who do not make money. In spring, of course, the lovers return; clandestine couples find shelter under lime trees, in flowered nooks; tourists photograph statues. But in winter, it's something else altogether.

Around the icy slide there are nannies and their army of children. Wrapped up in cumbersome padded jackets, the toddlers run like fat Japanese dolls, noses trickling snot, fingers violet. They breathe out white steam and stare at it, fascinated. In strollers, babies held tight under straps contemplate their elder siblings. Perhaps some of them feel melancholic, impatient. They probably can't wait to be able to get warm by crawling up the wooden climbing frame. They are eager to escape the surveillance of these women who catch them with a sure or rough hand, their voices calm or furious. Women wearing bou-bous on this freezing winter day.

There are mothers too, mothers staring into space. Like the one who gave birth recently and now finds her-self confined to the world's edge; who, sitting on this bench, feels the weight of her still flabby belly. She carries her body of pain and secretions, her body that smells of sour milk and blood. This flesh that she drags around with her, which she gives no care or rest. There are smiling, ra-diant mothers, those extremely rare mothers, gazed at lovingly by all the children. The ones who did not say good-bye this morning, who didn't leave them in the arms of another. The ones set free by a day off work, who have come here to enjoy it, bringing a strange enthusiasm to this ordinary winter's day at the park.

There are some men too, but closer to the benches, closer to the sandpit, closer to the little ones, the women form a solid wall, an impassable barrier. They are suspicious of men who come near, who take an interest in this world of women. They drive away the men who smile at the children, who stare at their plump cheeks and their little legs. The grandmothers deplore this: "All those pedophiles around nowadays! That didn't exist, in my day."

Louise does not let Mila out of her sight. The little girl runs from the slide to the swings. She never stops, because she doesn't want to get cold. Her gloves are soaked and she wipes them on her pink coat. Adam sleeps in his stroller. Louise has wrapped him up in a blanket and she gently strokes the skin on the back of his neck, between the top of his sweater and the bottom of his woolly hat. The metallic glare of an icy sun makes her squint.

"Want one?"

A young woman sits next to her, legs apart. She holds out a little jar in which honey candies are stuck together. Louise looks at her. She can't be more than twenty-five and there is something vulgar about the way she smiles. Her long black hair is dirty and unkempt, but you can tell that she could be pretty. Or attractive, anyway. She has sensual curves, a slightly round belly, thick thighs. She chews her candies with her mouth open and noisily sucks her honey-covered fingers.

"No, thank you." Louise refuses the offer with a wave of her hand.

"Where I come from, we always share our food with strangers. It's only here that I've seen people eating on their own." A boy of about four comes over to the young woman and she sticks a candy in his mouth. The little boy laughs.

"It's good for you," she tells him. "But it's a secret, okay? We won't tell your mother."

The little boy is called Alphonse, and Mila likes playing with him. Louise comes to the park every day and every day she refuses the fatty pastries that Wafa offers her. She tells Mila she mustn't eat any either, but Wafa doesn't take offense. The young woman is very chatty and on that bench, her hip pressed against Louise, she tells the nanny her life story. Mostly she talks about men.

Wafa reminds her of a big cat, not too subtle but very resourceful. She doesn't have her official papers yet, but doesn't seem worried about it. She arrived in France thanks to an old man to whom she used to give massages in a seedy hotel in Casablanca. The man became fond of her hands, so soft, then of her mouth and of her buttocks and, finally, of her entire body, which she offered him, following both her instinct and her mother's advice. The old man brought her to Paris, where he lived in a shabby apartment and received welfare. "He was scared that I'd get pregnant and his children pressured him into kicking me out. But the old man, he wanted me to stay."

Faced with Louise's silence, Wafa talks as if she's confessing to a priest or the police. She tells the nanny the details of a life that will never be recorded. After leaving the old man's apartment, she was recruited by a woman who signed her up for dating sites aimed at young Muslim women who were illegal immigrants. One evening a man arranged to meet her in a local McDonald's. The man thought she was beautiful. He made advances. He even tried to rape her. She managed to calm him down. They started talking money. Youssef agreed to marry her for twenty thousand euros. "That's cheap for getting your French papers," he explained.

She found this job—a godsend—with a French-American couple. They treat her well, even if they're very demanding. They rented her a studio just around the corner from where they live. "They pay my rent, but in exchange I can never say no to them."

"I adore this kid!" she says, staring greedily at Alphonse. Louise and Wafa fall silent. An icy wind sweeps through the park and they know that they will soon have to leave. "Poor little boy. Look at him, he can hardly move cos I've wrapped him up so warm. If he catches a cold, his mother will kill me."

Wafa sometimes feels afraid that she will grow old in one of these parks. That she'll feel her knees crack on these old frozen benches, that she won't be strong enough to lift up a child anymore. Alphonse will grow up. Soon he won't set foot in a park on a winter afternoon. He'll follow the sun. He'll go on vacation. Perhaps one day he'll sleep in one of the rooms of the Grand Hotel, where she used to massage men. This boy she raised will be serviced by one of her sisters or her cousins, on the terrace with its yellow and blue tiles.

"You see? Everything turns around and upside down. His childhood and my old age. My youth and his life as a man. Fate is vicious as a reptile. It always ends up pushing us to the wrong side of the handrail."

The rain starts to fall. Time to leave.

For Paul and Myriam, the winter flies past. During those few weeks, they see very little of each other. They meet in bed, one joining the other in sleep. Their feet touch under the sheets; one kisses the other's neck and laughs at hearing the other mumble like an animal disturbed in its sleep. They call each other during the day, leave messages. Myriam writes loving Post-it notes that she sticks to the bathroom mirror. In the middle of the night, Paul sends her videos of his rehearsals.

Life has become a succession of tasks, commitments to honor, appointments to keep. Myriam and Paul are snowed under with work. They like to repeat this as if their exhaustion was a portent of success. Their life is full to bursting; there's hardly even time for sleep, never mind thinking. They rush from one place to another, change shoes in taxis, have drinks with people who are important for their careers. The two of them have become the heads of a booming business, a business with clear objectives, an income stream, expenses.

All over the apartment, there are lists that Myriam

has written—on a paper napkin, on a Post-it, on the last page of a book. She spends her time looking for them. She is afraid to throw them away as if this might make her lose track of all the tasks she has to accomplish. She has kept some really old ones and, rereading them, she feels a nostalgia that is only intensified when she can no longer remember to what those obscure notes refer.

> Pharmacy
> Tell Mila Nils's story
> Reservations for Greece
> Call M.
> Reread all my notes
> Go back to that shop. Buy the dress?
> Reread Maupassant
> Get him a surprise?

Paul is happy. His life, for once, seems to be living up to his appetite for it, his insane energy levels, his joie de vivre. The boy who grew up in the great wide open is finally able to spread out. In a few months, his career has changed beyond all recognition, and for the first time in his life he is doing exactly what he wants. He no longer spends his days serving others, obeying and keeping silent, confronted with a hysterical producer, a group of infantile singers. Gone are his days of waiting for artists who turn up six hours late without bothering to warn him. Gone those recording sessions with aging MOR singers or the ones who need liters of alcohol and dozens of lines before they can play a note. Paul spends his nights at the studio, avid for music, new ideas, hysterical laughter. He doesn't leave anything to chance, spends hours correcting the sound of a snare drum, a drum arrangement. "Louise is there!" he always tells his wife when she worries about their absences.

When Myriam first got pregnant he was thrilled, but he told his friends that he didn't want his life to change. Myriam thought he was right, and she looked at her man—so sporty, so handsome, so independent—with even more admiration. He had promised her he would make sure that their life remained luminous and full of surprises. "We'll travel and we'll take the kid with us. You'll become a great lawyer, I'll produce records by acclaimed artists, and nothing will change." They pretended; they tried.

In the months that followed Mila's birth, life turned into a rather sad act. Myriam concealed the rings around her eyes and her melancholy. She was afraid of admitting to herself that she was sleepy all the time. Around that period, Paul started asking her: "What are you thinking about?" and each time she felt like crying. They invited friends to their apartment and Myriam had to force herself not to throw them out, not to knock the table over, not to lock herself in her bedroom. Their friends laughed; they raised their glasses and Paul refilled them. They argued and Myriam worried about her daughter being woken. She could have screamed from tiredness.

After Adam's birth it was even worse. The night they came home from the maternity ward, Myriam fell asleep in the bedroom, the transparent cradle next to her. Paul couldn't sleep. It seemed to him that there was a strange smell in the apartment. The same smell as in pet stores, on the docks, where he sometimes took Mila on weekends. A smell of secretion and confinement, of dried piss in a litter tray. That smell sickened him. He got up and took the trash outside. He opened the window. And then he realized that it was Mila who had thrown everything she could find in the toilets, which were now overflowing, spreading that foul wind throughout the apartment.

During that period Paul felt trapped, overwhelmed by obligations. He became a pale shadow of his usual easygoing, optimistic self, the tall blond man with the booming laugh who made girls turn to watch him as he passed without him even noticing. He stopped having mad ideas, suggesting weekends in the mountains and trips in the car to eat oysters on the beach. He tempered his enthusiasms. In the months that followed Adam's birth he started avoiding the apartment. He invented meetings and drank beer, alone, in hiding, in a quarter far from home. His friends had become parents too, and most of them had left Paris for the suburbs, the provinces or warmer lands in the south of Europe. For a few months Paul became childish, irresponsible, ridiculous. He kept secrets and harbored desires of escape. And yet he made no allowances for himself. He knew just how banal his attitude was. All he wanted was not to go home, to be free, to live again. He realized now—too late—that he hadn't lived very much before this. The clothes of a father seemed at once too big for him and too sad.

But it was done now, and he couldn't say that he didn't want it anymore. The children were there—loved, adored, unconditionally—but doubt was insinuating itself everywhere. The children, their smell, their gestures, their desire for him: all of this touched him to a degree that he would never be able to describe. Sometimes he wanted to be a kid too, to put himself in their shoes, to dissolve into childhood. Something was dead and it wasn't only youth or the feeling of being carefree. He wasn't useless anymore. They needed him and he was going to have to deal with that. By becoming a father, he had acquired principles and certainties, things he had sworn never to have. His generosity had become relative. His passions had grown tepid. His world had shrunk.

Louise is there now and Paul has started arranging dates with his wife again. One afternoon he sent her a message. "Place des Petits-Pères." She didn't reply and he found her silence wonderful. Like a form of politeness; a lover's silence. His heart was racing when he arrived in the square, slightly early, slightly worried. "She'll come. Of course she'll come." She came and they walked on the docks, like they used to do, before.

He knows how much they need Louise, but he can't stand her anymore. With her doll's body, her irritating habits, she really gets on his nerves. "She's so perfect, so delicate, that sometimes it sickens me," he admitted to Myriam one day. He is horrified by her little-girl figure, that way she has of dissecting every little thing the children do or say. He despises her dubious theories on education and her grandmotherly methods. He ridicules the photographs she has started sending them from her mobile phone, ten times a day, showing the children smiling as they lift up their empty plates, with the caption: "I ate it all."

Since the incident with the makeup, he talks to her as little as possible. That evening he even thought about firing her. He called Myriam to discuss the idea with her. She was in the office, and she didn't have time. So he waited until she got home and when his wife came through the door, about 11 p.m., he told her what had happened, the way Louise had looked at him, her icy silence, her arrogance.

Myriam reasoned with him. She played down the episode. She blamed him for having been too hard on the nanny, for having hurt her feelings. But then, they are always in league against him, like two bears. When it comes to the children, they sometimes treat him with a haughtiness that makes him bristle. They act like mothers, treat him like a child.

Sylvie, Paul's mother, made fun of them. "You act like the big bosses with your governess. Don't you think you're overdoing it?" Paul became annoyed. His parents had raised him to detest money and power, and to have a slightly mawkish respect for those "below" him. He had always been relaxed in his job, working with people with whom he felt equal. He had always called his boss *tu*, not *vous*. He had never given orders. But Louise had turned him into a boss. He hears himself giving his wife despicable advice. "Don't make too many concessions, otherwise she'll never stop asking for more," he says, widening his hands apart.

In the bath, Myriam is playing with her son. She holds him between her thighs, presses him against her and cuddles him so tightly that Adam ends up struggling and crying. She can't stop herself kissing him all over his chubby, perfect cherub's body. She looks at him and feels a gust of hot maternal love blow over her. She thinks that soon she won't dare to be like this with him, the two of them naked and close together. That it won't happen anymore. And then, faster than seems possible, she will be old and he—this laughing, pampered child—will be a man.

As she was undressing him, she noticed two strange marks, on his arm and at the top of his back. Two red scars, almost vanished, but where she can still make out what look like tooth marks. She gently kisses these wounds. She holds her son against her. She asks him to forgive her and belatedly consoles him for the sadness he felt at her absence.

The next morning, Myriam talks to Louise about it. The nanny has just entered the apartment. She hasn't even had time to take off her coat before Myriam is holding out

Adam's bare little arm toward her. Louise does not appear surprised.

She raises her eyebrows, hangs up her coat and asks: "Has Paul taken Mila to school?"

"Yes, they just left. Louise, did you see? That's a bite mark, isn't it?"

"Yes, I know. I put a bit of cream on it to help it heal. It was Mila who bit him."

"Are you sure? Were you there? Did you see it?"

"Of course I was there. The two of them were playing in the living room while I made dinner. And then I heard Adam screaming. He was sobbing, poor thing, and to start with I couldn't work out why. Mila bit him through his clothes: that's why I didn't know straightaway."

"I don't understand," Myriam says, kissing Adam's hairless head. "I asked her several times if it was her. I even told her I wouldn't punish her. She swore to me that she didn't know where that bite came from."

Louise sighs. She lowers her head. She looks as if she's hesitating.

"I promised not to say anything, and I really don't like the idea of breaking a promise I made to a child."

She takes off her black cardigan, unbuttons her shirt-dress and exposes her shoulder. Myriam leans in close and is unable to hold back a gasp of surprise and disgust. She stares at the brown mark that covers Louise's shoulder. It's an old scar, but she can clearly see the shapes of the little teeth that bit into the flesh, lacerating it.

"Mila did that to you?"

"Listen, I promised Mila I wouldn't say anything. Please don't talk to her about it. If the bond of trust between us was broken, I think she'd be even more disturbed. Do you see?"

"Ah."

"She's a bit jealous of her brother. That's completely normal. Leave me to deal with it, okay? You'll see, everything will be fine."

"Yeah. Maybe. But honestly, I don't understand."

"You shouldn't try to understand everything. Children are just like adults. There's nothing to understand."

How gloomy she looked, Louise, when Myriam told her that they were going to the mountains for a week to stay with Paul's parents! Myriam thinks about it again now, and she shivers. A storm flickered behind Louise's dark glare. That evening the nanny left without saying good-bye to the children. Like a ghost, monstrously discreet, she banged the door shut behind her and Mila and Adam said: "Mama, Louise has disappeared."

A few days later, on the eve of their departure, Sylvie came to fetch them. Louise had not been prepared for this. The cheerful, eccentric grandmother shouted as she came into the apartment. She threw her bag on the floor and rolled in the bed with the children, promising them a week of parties, games and gluttony. When she turned away, Myriam laughed at her mother-in-law's tomfoolery. Standing in the kitchen, Louise watched them. The nanny was deathly pale and her eyes, encircled by dark rings, looked sunken. She seemed to be mumbling something. Myriam moved toward her but Louise crouched down to fasten a suitcase. Later Myriam told herself that she must have been imagining things.

Myriam tries to calm herself. She has no reason to feel guilty. She doesn't owe her nanny anything. And yet, without being able to explain it, she has the feeling that she is tearing the children away from Louise, refusing her something. Punishing her.

Perhaps Louise was upset at being informed so late, not having time to organize her vacations. Or maybe she's just annoyed that the children are spending time with Sylvie, whom she doesn't like at all. When Myriam complains about her mother-in-law, the nanny tends to lose her temper. She takes Myriam's side with excessive zeal, accusing Sylvie of being mad, hysterical, of being a bad influence on the children. She encourages her boss not to let it happen; or, worse, to distance the grandmother from the poor children. In those moments, Myriam feels simultaneously supported and slightly uneasy.

As he is about to start the car, Paul takes off the watch from his left wrist.

"Can you put this in your bag, please?" he asks Myriam.

He bought this watch two months ago, paying for it with the money received from a contract with a famous singer. It's a secondhand Rolex that a friend found for him at a very reasonable price. Paul agonized before acquiring it. He really wanted it—he thought it was perfect—but he felt slightly ashamed of this fetishism, this frivolous desire. The first time he wore it, the watch seemed both beautiful and enormous. He found it too heavy, too flashy. He kept pulling down the sleeve of his jacket to conceal it. But very soon he got used to this weight at the end of his left arm. Really, this piece of jewelry—the first he'd ever possessed—was fairly discreet. And anyway, he had a right to treat himself. He hadn't stolen it from anyone.

"Why are you taking off your watch?" Myriam asks him, knowing how fond of it he is. "Has it stopped working?"

"No, it works fine. But you know my mother. She wouldn't understand. And I don't feel like spending the whole evening being told off for that."

It is early evening when they arrive. The house is freezing, and half of its rooms are still being renovated. The kitchen ceiling looks like it's about to collapse and there are bare electrical wires in the bathroom. Myriam hates this place. She is fearful for the children. She follows them all over the house, eyes full of panic, hands ready to stop them from falling. She prowls. She interrupts their games. "Mila, come and put another sweater on." "Adam's breathing strangely, don't you think?"

One morning, she wakes up numb. She breathes on Adam's frozen hands. She worries about Mila's paleness and forces her to keep her hat on in the house. Sylvie prefers not to say anything. She would like to give the children the wildness and whimsy that they are forbidden. There are no rules with her. She doesn't shower them with foolish gifts, like parents trying to compensate for their absences. She doesn't pay attention to the words she uses and she is constantly reprimanded for this by Paul and Myriam.

To annoy her daughter-in-law, she compares the children to "little birds fallen out of their nest." She likes to feel sorry for them having to live in a city, having to put up with rudeness and pollution. She would like to widen the horizons of these children doomed to become sensible, middle-class people, at once servile and authoritarian. Doomed to be cowards.

Sylvie bites her tongue. She does her best not to broach the subject of the children's education. A few months before this, the two women had argued violently. The kind of argument that time does not erase, its words still echoing inside them for a long time afterward whenever they see each other. Everyone had been drinking. Way too much. Myriam, feeling sentimental, had sought a compassionate ear from Sylvie. She complained about never seeing the children, about suffering from this frantic existence where no one ever gave her an easy ride. But Sylvie did not console her. She did not put her hand on Myriam's shoulder. On the contrary, she launched an all-out attack on her daughter-in-law. Her knives, apparently, were well sharpened, ready to be used when the occasion presented itself. Sylvie reproached her for devoting too much time to her job, despite the fact that she herself had worked all the way through Paul's childhood and had always boasted about her independence. She called her irresponsible and selfish. She counted on her fingers the number of work trips that Myriam had made even while Adam was ill and

Paul was finishing the recording of an album. It was her fault, Sylvie said, if her children had become unbearable, tyrannical, capricious. Her fault and also the fault of Louise, that phony nanny, that fake mother on whom Myriam depended, out of complacency, out of cowardice. Myriam started crying. Paul, stunned, did not say a word, and Sylvie waved her arms in the air as she shouted: "Go ahead and cry! Look at her. She cries and we're supposed to feel sorry for her because she's incapable of hearing the truth."

Every time that Myriam sees Sylvie, the memory of that evening oppresses her. That night, she felt as if she were being assaulted, thrown to the ground and stabbed repeatedly with a dagger. Myriam lay there, her guts slashed open, in front of her husband. She didn't have the strength to defend herself against those accusations, which she knew were partly true but which she considered as her lot and that of many other women. Not for an instant was there even a hint of clemency or gentleness. Not a single piece of advice was offered from mother to mother, from woman to woman.

Over breakfast, Myriam stares fixedly at her telephone. She tries desperately to check her emails, but the service is too slow and she gets so furious that she wants to throw her phone at the wall. Hysterical, she threatens Paul that she will go back to Paris. Sylvie raises her eyebrows, visibly exasperated. She had always hoped that her son would find a different kind of woman, more outdoorsy, more whimsical. A girl who loved nature, hiking in the mountains; a girl who wouldn't complain about the discomforts of this charming house.

For a long time Sylvie used to ramble on, always telling the same stories about her youth, her past political commitments, her revolutionary comrades. With age, she learned to tone this down. Essentially, she realized that no one cared about her nebulous theories on this world of sellouts, this world of arrant morons addicted to electronic screens and slaughtered animals. When she was their age, her only dream was of revolution. "We were a bit naive, though," suggests Dominique, her husband, who is saddened to see her unhappy. "Naive? Maybe, but we weren't as stupid as them." She knows that her husband doesn't understand her ideals, which are mocked by everyone. He listens kindly as she unloads her disappointments and anxieties. She laments what her son has become—"He was such a carefree little boy, you remember?"—a man trapped under his wife's thumb, a slave to her lust for money and her vanity. For a long time, she believed that a revolution led by both sexes would give birth to a very different world, where her grandchildren would grow up. A world where there would be time to live. "Darling, you're naive," Dominique tells her. "Women are capitalists, just like men."

Myriam paces around the kitchen, phone in hand. To soothe the tension, Dominique suggests they go for a walk. Myriam, calming down, wraps up her children in three layers of sweaters, scarves and gloves. Outside in the snow, Mila and Adam run around, ecstatic. Sylvie has brought two old sledges, which belonged to Paul and his brother Patrick when they were children. Myriam makes an effort not to worry and she watches, breath held, as the little ones speed down a slope.

They'll break their necks, she thinks, and I'll cry about it. She constantly tells herself: Louise would understand how I feel.

Paul is enthusiastic. He encourages Mila, who waves at him and says: "Look, Papa. Look, I'm sledging!" They eat lunch at a pleasant inn, a fire crackling in the hearth. They sit near the window, and shafts of dazzling sunlight shine on the children's pink cheeks. Mila is talkative and she makes the adults laugh with her silliness. Adam, for once, eats heartily.

That evening Myriam and Paul take the exhausted children up to their bedroom. Mila and Adam are calm, their limbs weak, their souls filled with happiness and new discoveries. The parents linger near them. Paul sits on the floor and Myriam on the edge of Mila's bed. She gently tucks her in, caresses her hair. For the first time in a long time, Myriam and Paul sing a lullaby together. They learned the words to it when Mila was born and they used to sing it to her in a duet when she was a baby. The children's eyes are closed, but the grown-ups keep singing for the pleasure of accompanying their dreams. So they don't have to leave them.

Paul doesn't dare say this to his wife but, that night, he feels relieved. Since coming to his parents' house, a weight seems to have lifted from his chest. Half-asleep, numb with cold, he thinks about going back to Paris. He imagines his apartment as an aquarium invaded by rotting seaweed, an airless pit where animals with balding fur prowl endlessly, groaning.

Back home, these dark thoughts are quickly forgotten. In the living room, Louise has arranged a bouquet of dahlias. Dinner is ready, the sheets smell clean. After a week in freezing beds, eating chaotic meals at the kitchen table, they are happy to return to their family comforts. It would be impossible, they think, to manage without her. They react like spoiled children, like purring cats.

A few hours after Paul and Myriam's departure, Louise retraces her footsteps and goes back up Rue d'Hauteville. She enters the Massés' apartment and opens the shutters that Myriam had closed. She changes all the sheets, empties the cupboards and dusts the shelves. She shakes out the old Berber rugs that Myriam refuses to get rid of, and vacuums the floors.

Her chores accomplished, she sits on the sofa and dozes. She doesn't leave the apartment all week and spends each day in the living room, with the television on. She never sleeps in Paul and Myriam's bed. She lives on the sofa. In order not to spend any money, she eats whatever she finds in the fridge and makes a start on the reserves in the pantry; Myriam probably has no idea what's in there anyway.

Cookery programs give way to the news, game shows, reality TV shows, a talk show that makes her laugh. She falls asleep in front of a true-crime show called *Enquêtes Criminelles*. One evening she watches an episode about a man found dead in a house on the outskirts of a small mountain town. The shutters were closed for months, the letterbox was overflowing, and yet no one wondered what had become of the house's owner. It was only when the neighborhood was being evacuated that some firemen finally opened the door and discovered the corpse. The body was practically mummified, due to the cold, stale air. Several times the voice-over mentions that it was possible to calculate the date of the man's death only because of some yogurts found in the fridge that were several months past their expiration date.

One afternoon Louise wakes with a start. She had been in one of those sleeps so heavy that they leave you feeling sad, disorientated, your stomach full of tears. A sleep so deep, so dark, that you see yourself dying, that you wake up soaked with cold sweat, paradoxically exhausted. In a panic, she sits up, slaps her own face. Her head aches so badly that she can hardly open her eyes. She can almost hear the sound of her heart thudding. She looks for her shoes. She slips on the floorboards, weeps with rage. She is late. The children will be waiting for her; the school will call; the nursery will notify Myriam of her absence. How could she have fallen asleep? How could she have been so careless? She has to leave, she has to run, but she can't find the apartment keys. She looks everywhere and finally spots them by the fireplace. In the stairway, the front door bangs shut behind her. Outside, she has the feeling that everyone is staring at her and she sprints along the streets, out of breath, like a madwoman. She puts her hand on her side;

she has a stitch and it's killing her, but she doesn't slow down.

There's no one to help her cross the road. Normally there's always someone in a fluorescent vest, holding a little sign. Either that young man with bad teeth whom she suspects has just got out of prison, or that tall black woman who knows all the children's names. There's no one outside the school either. Louise stands there alone, like an idiot. A bitter taste stings her tongue. She wants to throw up. The children aren't there. She walks with her head lowered now, in tears. The children are on vacation. She's alone; she'd forgotten. She hits her own forehead anxiously.

Wafa calls her several times a day, "just for a chat." One evening she asks if she can come around to see Louise. Her bosses are away on vacation too and for once she is free to do what she wants. Louise wonders what Wafa wants from her. She finds it hard to believe that anyone could be so desperate for her company. But she is still haunted by her nightmare from the day before and she agrees.

She arranges to meet her friend outside the Massés' apartment building. In the lobby, Wafa talks loudly about the surprise that she has for Louise, hidden inside the large woven-plastic bag she is carrying. Louise shushes her. She is afraid that someone will hear them. Solemnly she climbs the stairs and opens the door to the apartment. The living room strikes her as heartbreakingly sad and she presses her palms to her eyes. She wants to retrace her steps, to get rid of Wafa, to return to the television which spits out its reassuring swill of images. But Wafa has put her plastic bag on the kitchen countertop and she takes from it some packets of spices, a chicken and one of the glass jars containing her honey candies. "I'm going to cook for you, okay?"

For the first time in her life, Louise sits on the sofa and watches someone make her a meal. Even as a child, she doesn't remember ever seeing anyone do that, just for her, just to make her happy. As a little girl, she used to eat other people's leftovers. She was given lukewarm soup in the morning, a soup that was reheated day after day until every last drop of it was gone. She had to eat all of it despite the cold fat stuck to the sides of the bowl, despite that taste of sour tomatoes, gnawed bones.

Wafa pours her a vodka mixed with ice-cold apple juice. "I like alcohol when it's sweetened," she says, clinking her glass against Louise's. Wafa is still standing. She picks up the ornaments, looks at the shelves of the bookcase. A photograph catches her eye.

"Is that you? You're pretty in that orange dress." In the photograph Louise is smiling, her hair loose. She is sitting on a low wall, holding a child in each arm. Myriam insisted on putting that picture in the living room, on one of the shelves. "You're part of the family," she told the nanny.

Louise remembers clearly the moment when Paul took that photograph. Myriam had gone into a ceramics shop and she was struggling to make up her mind. Louise was looking after the children in the street lined with shops.

Mila stood on the wall. She was trying to catch a gray cat. That was when Paul said: "Louise, kids, look at me. The light's perfect." Mila sat next to Louise and Paul called out: "Now, smile!"

"This year," Louise says, "we're going back to Greece. There, to Sifnos," she adds, pointing at the photograph with her painted fingernail. They haven't talked about this yet, but Louise is certain that they will return to their island, swim in the clear sea and eat dinner on the port, by candlelight. Myriam makes lists, she explains to Wafa, who sits on the floor, at her friend's feet. Lists that she leaves in the living room, even in the sheets of their bed, and she wrote on those lists that they will go back there soon. They will go for walks in rocky inlets. They will trap crabs, sea urchins and sea cucumbers that Louise will watch shrinking at the bottom of a bucket. She will swim, farther and farther out, and this year Adam will join her.

And then, the end of the vacation will draw closer. The day before they return to Paris, they will probably go to that restaurant that Myriam loved so much, where the boss had let the children choose which fish they wanted. There they will drink a bit of wine and Louise will announce her decision not to go back with them. "I'm not going to catch the plane tomorrow. I'm going to live here." Of course, they will be surprised. They won't take her seriously. They'll start laughing, because they'll have had too much to drink or because they're feeling ill at ease. And then, faced with the nanny's resolve, they will start to worry. They will try to talk her around. "Come on, Louise, that makes no sense. You can't stay here. And how will you make a living?" And then it will be Louise's turn to laugh.

"Obviously, I thought about winter." The island must look very different then. These dry rocky hills, these oregano bushes, these thistles must look quite hostile in the November gloom. It must be dark, up there, when the first rains fall. But she won't change her mind: no one will persuade her to return to France. She'll move to a different island, perhaps, but she will never go back.

"Or maybe I won't tell them anything. I'll just disappear, like that," she says, snapping her fingers.

Wafa listens to Louise talk about her plans. She has no trouble imagining those blue horizons, those cobbled streets, those morning swims. She feels terribly homesick. Louise's words awaken memories, the salty smell of the Atlantic in the evening from the coast road, the sunrises greeted by the whole family during Ramadan. But Louise suddenly starts laughing, shattering Wafa's sweet daydream. She laughs like a shy little girl who hides her teeth behind her fingers and she reaches out her hand to her friend, who sits next to her on the sofa. They raise their glasses and make a toast. They look like two young girls now, two schoolmates sharing a private joke, or a secret. Like two children, lost in an adult world.

Wafa has maternal or sisterly instincts. She thinks about getting Louise a drink of water, making her coffee, making her something to eat. Louise stretches out her legs and crosses her feet on the table. Wafa looks at Louise's dirty sole next to her glass, and she thinks that her friend must be drunk to act like that. She has always admired

Louise's manners, her prim politeness, which could pass for that of a real bourgeois lady. Wafa puts her bare feet on the edge of the table. And in a salacious voice, she says: "Maybe you'll meet someone on your island? A handsome Greek man, who'll fall in love with you . . ."

"Oh, no," replies Louise. "If I go there, it's so I don't have to look after anyone anymore. So I can sleep when I want, eat whatever I like."

To begin with, the plan was not to do anything for Wafa's wedding. They would just go to the town hall, sign the documents, and each month Wafa would pay Youssef what she owed him until she had her French papers. But her future husband ended up changing his mind. He suggested to his mother, who was only too willing to comply, that it would be more decent to invite a few friends. "I mean, it is my wedding. Anyway, you never know, it might help convince the immigration services."

One Friday morning they arrange to meet outside the town hall in Noisy-le-Sec. Louise, who is a witness for the first time, wears her sky-blue Peter Pan collar and a pair of earrings. She signs at the bottom of the sheet that the mayor hands her and the wedding seems almost real. The hoorays, the cries of "Here's to the happy couple!," the applause . . . all of it sounds sincere.

The little group walks to the restaurant, La Gazelle d'Agadir, run by a friend of Wafa's, and where she has sometimes worked as a waitress. Louise observes the other guests, who stand around gesticulating, laughing and slapping one another on the shoulder. Outside the restaurant, Youssef's brothers have parked a black sedan with dozens of gold plastic ribbons attached to it.

The restaurant owner has put music on. He's not worried about the neighbors; on the contrary, he thinks it will be good publicity for his restaurant, that people passing in the street will look through the window at the elegantly set tables, that they will envy the guests' happiness. Louise observes the women; she is particularly struck by their broad faces, their thick hands, their wide hips accentuated by belts tied too tight. They speak loudly, they laugh, they call across the room at one another. They surround Wafa, who is sitting at the table of honor and who, Louise gathers, is not allowed to move.

Louise has been seated at the end of the room, far from the window that overlooks the street, next to a man whom Wafa had introduced her to this morning. "I told you about Hervé. He did some work in my studio. He works quite nearby." Wafa deliberately seated her next to him. He is the kind of man she deserves. A man no one wants but who Louise will take, the way she takes old clothes, secondhand magazines with pages missing, even waffles half-eaten by the children.

She is not attracted to Hervé. She is embarrassed by Wafa's knowing looks. She hates this sensation of being spied on, trapped. And besides, this man is so ordinary. There is so little about him to like. For a start, he is barely any taller than Louise. His legs are muscular but short and his hips are narrow. Hardly any neck. When he speaks, he sometimes pulls his head back into his shoulders, like a shy turtle. Louise keeps staring at his hands as they rest on the table: they are a working man's hands, a poor man's hands, a smoker's hands. She has noticed that he has teeth missing. He is not distinguished. He smells of cucumber and wine. The first thing she thinks is that she would be ashamed to introduce him to Myriam and Paul. They would be disappointed. She is sure that they would think this man isn't good enough for her.

Hervé, on the other hand, stares at Louise with the eagerness of an old man for a young woman who has shown a bit of interest in him. He finds her so elegant, so delicate. He notes the slenderness of her neck, the lightness of her earrings. He observes her hands as they writhe in her lap, her little white hands with pink fingernails, her hands that look as if they have not suffered, not been worked to the bone. Louise reminds him of those porcelain dolls he's seen sitting on shelves in the apartments of old ladies where he has gone to do a favor or do some work. Like those dolls, Louise's features are almost motionless; sometimes her frozen expression is absolutely beautiful. She has a way of staring into space that makes Hervé want to remind her of his existence.

He tells her about his job. He's a delivery driver, but not full-time. He also does odd jobs, repairs things, helps people move house. Three days a week he works as a security guard in the parking lot of a bank, on Boulevard Haussmann. "It gives me time to read," he says. "Thrillers mostly, but not always." She doesn't know what to say when he asks her what she reads.

"What about music, then? Do you like music?"

He is mad about it and, with his little purple fingers, he pretends to pluck the strings of a guitar. He talks about life before, in the old days, when people listened to music all the time, when singers were idols. He used to have long hair and worship Jimi Hendrix. "I'll show you a photo," he says. Louise realizes that she has never listened to music. She never got a taste for it. All she knows are nursery rhymes, simple rhyming songs passed on from mother to daughter. One evening, Myriam heard her humming a tune with the children. She told her she had a very nice voice. "It's a shame, you could have been a singer."

Louise has not noticed that most of the guests are not drinking alcohol. In the center of each table there is a bottle of soda and a large carafe of water. Hervé has hidden a bottle of wine on the floor, to his right, and he pours more into Louise's glass whenever it's empty. She drinks slowly. She ends up getting used to the deafening music, the yelling of the guests, the incomprehensible speeches of the young men who talk with their lips too close to the microphone. She even smiles as she watches Wafa and she forgets that all of this is nothing but a masquerade, a fool's game, a hoax.

She drinks and the discomfort of living, the shyness of breathing, all this anguish dissolves in the liquid she sips. The banality of the restaurant, and of Hervé . . . it is all transformed. Hervé has a soft voice and he knows when to shut up. He looks at her and he smiles, eyes lowered to the table. When he has nothing to say, he says nothing. His little lashless eyes, his sparse hair, his purplish skin, his manners no longer displease Louise so much.

She lets Hervé walk her to the metro station. She says good-bye and walks down the steps without turning around. On the way home, Hervé thinks about her. She inhabits him like a catchy song in English, a language he doesn't understand at all, and in which, despite all those years spent listening to music, he continues mangling his favorite choruses.

At 7:30, as she does every morning, Louise opens the front door of the apartment. Paul and Myriam are standing in the living room. They look as if they've been waiting for her. Myriam resembles a half-starved animal that has been prowling its cage all night. Paul turns on the television and, for once, lets the children watch cartoons before they go to school.

"Stay here. Don't move," he orders Mila and Adam, who stare hypnotized, mouths hanging open, at a group of hysterical rabbits.

The adults lock themselves in the kitchen. Paul asks Louise to sit down.

"Shall I make you a coffee?" the nanny asks.

"No, thanks, I'm fine," Paul replies coldly. Behind him, Myriam stares at the floor; her hand touches her lips. "Louise, we received a letter that has put us in a difficult position. I have to admit that we are very upset by what we learned. There are certain things that cannot be tolerated." He says all this in a single breath, his eyes riveted to the envelope in his hands.

Louise stops breathing. She can't even feel her tongue anymore and has to bite her lip to prevent herself crying. She wants to act like a child would: cover her ears, scream, roll on the floor, anything to avoid having this conversation. She tries to identify the letter that Paul is holding, but she can't make out anything: not the address, nor the contents.

Suddenly she feels sure that the letter is from Mrs. Grinberg. The old harpy was probably spying on her while Paul and Myriam were away, and now she is telling them everything. She's written a poison-pen letter, denouncing Louise, insulting her, as a way of distracting herself from her solitude. Undoubtedly she has told them how Louise spent her vacation here. That she invited Wafa. Maybe she even sent the letter anonymously, to add to the mystery, the malice. And besides, she probably invented things, covering the paper with all her old-lady fantasies, her lewd, senile delusions. Louise won't be able to stand it. No, she won't be able to stand the disgusted look on her boss's face, the idea that Myriam will believe that she slept in their bed, that she made fun of them behind their backs.

Louise stiffens. Her fingers are tensed with hate and she hides her hands behind her knees so Paul and Myriam won't see them shaking. Her face and throat are pale. In a rage, she puts her fingers through her hair. Paul, who was waiting for a reaction, goes on.

"This letter is from the tax office, Louise. They're asking us to take from your wages the sum that you owe them—and have apparently owed them for months. You've never replied to single reminder letter!"

Paul could swear he saw relief in the nanny's face.

"I'm well aware that this is humiliating for you, but it's not very pleasant for us either, you know."

Paul hands the letter to Louise, who does not move. "Look."

Louise takes the envelope and removes the sheet of paper from it, her hands clammy and trembling. Her vision is blurred. She pretends to read the letter, but she doesn't take in a word of it.

"If it's got to this point, it's their last resort, you understand? You can't act so negligently," Myriam explains.

"I'm sorry," she says. "I'm sorry, Myriam. I'll take care of this, I promise."

"I can help you, if you need help. You'll have to bring me all the documents so we can find a solution."

Louise rubs her cheek, palm open, eyes vacant. She knows she ought to say something. She would like to hug Myriam, to ask for her help. She would like to say that she is alone, completely alone, and that so many things have happened, so many things that she hasn't been able to tell anyone, but that she would like to tell her. She is upset, shaky. She doesn't know how to behave.

In the end Louise puts a brave face on it. She claims it is all a misunderstanding. Says something about a change of address. She blames Jacques, her husband, who was so careless and so secretive. She denies it, against all reality, against all the evidence. Her speech is so confused and pathetic that Paul rolls his eyes. "Okay, okay. It's your business, so deal with it. I don't ever want to receive this type of letter again."

The letters had pursued her from Jacques's house to

her studio flat and, finally, here, to her domain, in this household that is held together only by her. They sent her the unpaid bills for Jacques's treatment, the property tax and the fines for its late payment, and some other debts that she doesn't even recognize. She had thought naively that they would just give up if she didn't reply. That she could just play dead. She doesn't represent anything, after all, doesn't possess anything. What can it matter to them? Why do they need to hunt her down?

She knows where the letters are. A pile of envelopes that she has not thrown away, that she has kept under the electric meter. She wanted to burn them. In any case, she doesn't understand any of those interminable sentences, those tables that cover entire pages, those columns of numbers with a total that keeps increasing. It was like when she used to help Stéphanie do her homework. When it came to helping her with math questions, her daughter would laugh and taunt her: "What the hell do you know about it, anyway? You're stupid."

That evening, after putting the children in pajamas, Louise lingers in their bedroom. Myriam stands rigid in the entrance hall, waiting for her. "You can go now. We'll see you tomorrow." Louise wishes she could stay. She wishes she could sleep here, at the foot of Mila's bed. She wouldn't make any noise; she wouldn't disturb anyone. Louise doesn't want to go back to her studio. Every evening she gets home a little later, and when she walks in the street she keeps her eyes lowered, her chin covered by a scarf. She is afraid of bumping into her landlord, an old man with red hair and bloodshot eyes. A miser who only trusted her "because renting to a white in this neighborhood is practically unheard of." He must be regretting his decision now.

On the train, she grits her teeth to stop herself crying. An icy, insidious rain soaks into her coat, her hair. Heavy drops fall from porches and slide down the back of her neck, making her shiver. At the corner of her street, even though it's empty, she feels she is being watched. She turns around, but there's no one there. Then, in the darkness, between two cars, she spots a man squatting on his haunches. She sees his two naked thighs, his huge hands resting on his knees. In one hand he holds a newspaper. He looks at her. He does not appear hostile or embarrassed. She recoils, feeling suddenly nauseated. She wants to scream, to make someone else witness the spectacle. A man is shitting in her street, under her nose. A man who apparently has no shame left and must have got used to doing his business without any modesty or dignity.

Louise runs to the door of her building. She is trembling as she climbs the stairs. She cleans her entire apartment. She changes the sheets. She would like to wash herself, to stand under a jet of hot water for a long time, until she's warmed up, but a few days ago the shower collapsed—the rotten floorboards under the cubicle gave way—and now it is out of order. Since then she has been washing herself in the sink, with a washcloth. She shampooed her hair three days ago, sitting on the Formica chair.

Lying on her bed, she is unable to fall asleep. She can't stop thinking about that man in the shadows. She can't help imagining that, soon, that will be her. That she'll be on the street. That she will have to leave even this vile apartment and that she will shit in the street, like an animal.

The next morning, Louise can't get up. All night she's been feverish, to the point that her teeth chattered. Her throat is swollen and full of ulcers. Even her own saliva seems impossible to swallow. It's just after 7:30 when the telephone starts to ring. She doesn't answer. And yet she sees Myriam's name on the screen. She opens her eyes, reaches out to the phone and hangs up. She buries her face in the pillow.

The telephone rings again.

This time Myriam leaves a message. "Hello, Louise, I hope you're well. It's nearly eight o'clock. Mila has been ill since last night—she has a fever. I have a very important case today, as I told you, and I need to be in court. I hope everything's all right, and that nothing has happened. Call me back when you get this message. We're expecting you." Louise throws the phone to the foot of the bed and rolls herself up in the bedcovers. She tries to forget that she is thirsty and desperate to urinate. She doesn't want to move.

She has pushed her bed against the wall, closer to the feeble warmth of the radiator. Lying like this, her nose is almost pressed up to the windowpane. Eyes turned to the skeletal trees in the street, she can find no way out. She has the strange certainty that all struggle is futile. That all she can do is let events carry her away, wash over her, overwhelm her, while she remains passive and inert. The day before, she gathered all the envelopes. She opened them and tore up the letters, one by one. She threw the pieces in the sink and turned on the tap. Once they were wet, the scraps of paper stuck together, forming a foul paste that she watched disintegrate under the trickle of hot water. The telephone rings, again and again. Louise has covered it with a cushion, but the shrill ringing stops her falling back asleep.

In the apartment, Myriam paces around in a panic, her lawyer's robes draped on the stripy chair. "She's not coming back," she tells Paul. "This won't be the first time that a nanny has just vanished overnight. I've heard lots of stories like that." She tries calling her again, but in the face of Louise's silence she feels completely helpless. She blames Paul. She accuses him of having been too harsh, of treating Louise like a mere employee. "We humiliated her," she says.

Paul tries to reason with his wife. Perhaps Louise has a problem; something probably happened. She would never dare abandon them like this, without an explanation. And she's so attached to the children, she couldn't leave them without saying good-bye. "Instead of coming up with crackpot theories, you should find out her address. Look on her contract. If she doesn't answer in the next hour, I'll go to her apartment."

Myriam is crouched on the floor, going through the drawers, when the telephone rings. In a barely audible voice, Louise makes her excuses. She is so ill that she hasn't managed to get out of bed. She fell asleep this morning and didn't hear her phone ringing. At least ten times she repeats, "I'm sorry." Myriam is caught out by this simple explanation. She feels slightly ashamed not to have even thought of it: a straightforward health problem. As if Louise were infallible, her body immune to fatigue and illness. "I understand," Myriam replies. "Get some rest. We'll find another solution."

Paul and Myriam call friends, colleagues, family. Finally someone gives them the number of a female student who "can help out if you're desperate," and who, thankfully, agrees to go to their apartment straightaway. The girl—a pretty blonde of twenty—does not inspire much confidence in Myriam. After entering the apartment, she slowly takes off her high-heeled ankle boots. Myriam notices that she has a hideous tattoo on her neck. To every recommendation that Myriam makes, she replies "Yeah" without really seeming to understand, as if she just wants to get rid of this nervous, nagging boss. With Mila, who is dozing on the sofa, she overdoes the solicitude, acting like a worried mother when the truth is she is still a child herself.

But it's in the evening, when she goes home, that Myriam is overwhelmed. The apartment is in chaos. Toys are scattered all over the living-room floor. The dirty dishes have been tossed in the sink. There are dried-out mashed-carrot stains on the little table. The girl gets to her feet, as relieved as a prisoner freed from her cell. She stuffs the cash in her pocket and runs to the door, mobile in hand. Later Myriam finds a dozen hand-rolled cigarette stubs on the balcony and, on the blue chest of drawers in the children's bedroom, some chocolate ice cream that has melted, damaging the paintwork.

For three days Louise has nightmares. She doesn't sink into sleep but into a sort of perverse lethargy, where her thoughts become scrambled and her unease is intensified. At night she is inhabited by a silent screaming inside her that tears at her guts. Her blouse stuck to her chest, her teeth grinding, she hollows out a furrow in the sofa bed's mattress. She feels as if her face is being crushed under a boot heel, as if her mouth is full of dirt. Her hips twitch like a tadpole's tail. She is totally exhausted. She wakes up to drink and go to the toilet, then returns to her nest.

She emerges from sleep the way you might rise up from the depths after you have swum too far, when you are oxygen-deprived, the water is a black sticky magma, and you are praying that you still have enough air, enough strength to reach the surface and breathe in, greedily, at last.

In her little notebook with the flower-patterned cover, she noted the term used by a doctor at the Henri-Mondor hospital. "Delirious melancholia." Louise had thought that was beautiful; it seemed to bestow a touch of poetry and

155

escape on her sadness. She wrote it down in her strange handwriting, all twisted, slanting capital letters. On the pages of that little notebook, the words resemble those shaky wooden constructions that Adam builds with blocks purely for the pleasure of watching them collapse.

For the first time, she thinks about old age. About her body, which is starting to malfunction; about the movements that make her ache deep in her bones. About her growing medical expenses. And then the fear of growing old and sick, bedridden, terminal, in this apartment with its dirty windows. It has become an obsession. She hates this place. She can't stop thinking about the smell of damp coming from the shower cubicle. She can taste it in her mouth. All the joints, all the cracks are filled with a greenish mold, and no matter how furiously she scrubs at them, they grow back during the night, thicker than ever.

Hate rises up inside her. A hate that clashes with her servile urges, her childlike optimism. A hate that muddies everything. She is absorbed by a sad, confused dream. Haunted by the feeling that she has seen too much, heard too much of other people's privacy, a privacy she has never enjoyed herself. She has never had her own bedroom.

After two nights of anguish, she feels ready to start work again. She has lost weight and her girlish face, pale and gaunt, looks as if it's been beaten into a narrower shape. She does her hair and makeup. She calms herself with layers of mauve eyeshadow.

At 7:30 a.m., she opens the front door of the apartment on Rue d'Hauteville. Mila, in her blue pajamas, runs at the nanny and jumps into her arms. She says: "Louise, it's you! You came back!"

In his mother's arms, Adam struggles. He has heard Louise's voice, he has recognized her smell of talc, the light sound of her footsteps on the wooden floor. With his little hands, he pushes himself away from his mother's chest. Smiling, Myriam hands her child into Louise's loving arms.

In Myriam's refrigerator, there are boxes. Very small boxes, piled neatly on top of one another. There are bowls, covered in aluminum foil. On the plastic shelves are little slices of lemon, a stale cucumber end, a quarter of an onion whose smell pervades the kitchen as soon as you open the fridge door. A piece of cheese with nothing but the rind remaining. In the boxes Myriam finds a few peas that are no longer round or bright green. Three bits of ravioli. A spoonful of broth. A shred of turkey that wouldn't feed a sparrow, but which Louise carefully kept anyway.

Paul and Myriam joke about this. This mania of Louise's, this phobia of throwing away food, makes them laugh at first. The nanny scrapes out the last morsels from jam jars; she makes the children lick out their pots of yogurt. Her employers find this ludicrous and touching.

Paul makes fun of Myriam when she takes out the trash bags in the middle of the night because they contain leftover food or a toy of Mila's that they can't be bothered to fix. "You're scared of being told off by Louise—admit it!" he laughs, following her into the stairwell.

They find it amusing to watch Louise study, with great concentration, the junk mail from local shops that is delivered to their letterbox and which they are used to throwing away without a thought. The nanny collects coupons and proudly presents them to Myriam, who is ashamed to find this behavior idiotic. In fact, Myriam uses Louise as an example when she lectures her husband and children. "Louise is right. It's bad to waste food. There are children who have nothing to eat."

But after a few months, Louise's obsession becomes the subject of tension. Myriam complains about the nanny's inflexible attitude, her paranoia. "Let her search through our garbage if she wants! I don't have to justify myself to her," she tells Paul, who is convinced that they have to free themselves from Louise's power. Myriam stands firm. She refuses to let Louise give the children food that is past its expiration date. "Yes, even if it's only one day past. That's it, end of discussion."

One evening, not long after Louise has returned to work following her illness, Myriam comes home late. The apartment is in total darkness and Louise is waiting at the door, wearing her coat and holding her handbag. She mumbles good-bye and rushes downstairs. Myriam is too tired to think about this or feel troubled by it.

Louise is sulking? Oh, who cares!

She could collapse on the sofa and fall asleep fully dressed, with her shoes still on. But she moves toward the kitchen, to get herself a glass of wine. She feels like sitting in the living room for a moment, drinking some very cold white wine, smoking a cigarette and relaxing. If she wasn't afraid that she would wake the children, she might even take a bath.

She enters the kitchen and turns on the light. The room looks even cleaner than usual. There's a strong smell of soap in the air. The fridge door has been cleaned. Nothing has been left on the countertop. The extractor hood over the cooker is free of grease stains, and the handles on the cupboard doors have been sponged off. As for the window facing her, it is spotlessly, dazzlingly clean.

Myriam is about to open the fridge when she sees it. There, in the middle of the little table where the children and their nanny eat. A chicken carcass sits on a plate. A glistening carcass, without the smallest scrap of flesh hanging from its bones, not the faintest trace of meat. It looks as if it's been gnawed clean by a vulture or a stubborn, meticulous insect. Some kind of repulsive animal, anyway.

She stares at the brown skeleton, its round spine, its sharp bones, its smooth vertebrae. Is thighs have been torn off, but its twisted little wings are still there, the joints distended, close to breaking point. The shiny, yellowish cartilage resembles dried pus. Through the holes, between the small bones, Myriam sees the empty insides of the thorax, dark and bloodless. No meat remains, no organs, nothing on this skeleton that could rot, and yet it seems to Myriam that it is a putrescent carcass, a vile corpse that is festering and decaying before her eyes, here in the kitchen.

She is sure of it: she threw away that chicken this morning. The meat was no longer edible; she didn't want her children to get ill from eating it. She remembers clearly how she shook the plate over the trash can and how the creature fell, covered in gelatinous fat. It landed with a wet thud at the bottom of the trash and Myriam said, "Ugh." That smell, so early in the morning, made her feel sick.

Myriam moves closer to the creature, but she doesn't dare touch it. Louise can't have done this by mistake or out of forgetfulness. And certainly not as a joke. No, the carcass smells of washing liquid and sweet almond. Louise washed it in the sink; she cleaned it and put it there as an act of vengeance, like a baleful totem.

Later Mila told her mother exactly what happened. She was laughing and jumping around as she explained how Louise had taught them to eat with their fingers. Standing on their chairs, she and Adam had scratched away at the bones. The meat was dry and Louise let them drink big glasses of Fanta as they ate, so they wouldn't choke. She was very careful not to damage the skeleton and she never took her eyes off the creature. She told them that it was a game and that she would reward them if they followed the rules exactly. And when it was over, they were allowed to eat two lemon drops as a special treat.

HECTOR ROUVIER

It's been ten years, but Hector Rouvier vividly remembers Louise's hands. That was what he touched most often, her hands. They smelled like crushed petals and her nails were always polished. Hector squeezed those hands, held them against him; he felt them on the back of his neck when he watched a film on television. Louise's hands plunged into hot water and rubbed Hector's skinny body. They massaged soap bubbles in his hair, slid under his armpits, washed his penis, his belly, his bottom.

Lying on the bed, face buried in his pillow, he would lift up his pajama top to let Louise know that he was waiting for her to caress him. She would run her fingernails down his back and his skin would get goosebumps, and he'd shiver, and fall asleep, soothed and slightly ashamed, with a vague understanding of the strange excitation into which Louise's fingers had sent him.

On the way to school, Hector would hold very tight to the nanny's hands. As he got older and his palms grew bigger, he felt increasingly worried that he might crush Louise's bones, her biscuit-like, porcelain bones. The nanny's knuckles would crack inside the child's palm, and sometimes Hector thought that he was the one holding Louise's hand, helping her to cross the road.

No, Louise was never harsh. He doesn't remember ever seeing her get angry. He's sure of that; she never lifted a hand to him. Despite all the years he spent with her, his memories are vague, blurry. Louise's face seems distant to him; he isn't sure he would recognize her today if he happened to pass her in the street. But the feel of her cheek, soft and smooth; the smell of her powder, which she put on every morning and evening; the sensation of her beige tights on his child's face; the strange way she had of kissing him, sometimes using her teeth, biting him as if to signify the sudden savagery of her love, her desire to completely possess him. Yes, all this he remembers.

He hasn't forgotten her culinary talents either. The cakes she would bring with her when she met him at the school gates and the way she would rejoice in the little boy's gluttony. The taste of her tomato sauce; the way she would pepper the steaks that she hardly cooked at all; her creamy mushroom sauce . . . these are memories that he often evokes. A mythology linked to his childhood, of the world before frozen meals eaten in front of his computer screen.

He also remembers—or, rather, he thinks he remembers—that she was infinitely patient with him. With his parents, the ceremony of bedtime often went wrong. Anne Rouvier, his mother, would lose patience when Hector cried, begged her to leave the door open, asked for another story, a glass of water, swore that he'd seen a monster, that he was still hungry.

"I'm the same," Louise had confessed to him. "I'm afraid of falling asleep too." She indulged him when he had nightmares and sometimes she would stroke his temples for hours, her long, rose-scented fingers accompanying him on his journey toward sleep. She had persuaded her boss to leave a light on in the child's bedroom. "There's no point in terrifying him like that."

Yes, her departure had been a wrench. He missed her terribly, and he hated the young woman who replaced her, a student who would pick him up from school, who spoke English to him, who—in his mother's words—"stimulated him intellectually." He blamed Louise for abandoning him, for not keeping the impassioned promises she had made, for betraying those solemn oaths of everlasting love, after swearing to him that he was the only one and that no one could ever take his place. One day she wasn't there anymore and Hector didn't dare ask any questions. He wasn't able to mourn the woman who had left him because, even though he was only eight, he intuitively knew that this particular love was laughable, that people would make fun of him, and that anyone who felt sorry for him would be pretending.

Hector lowers his head. He stops talking. His mother is sitting on a chair next to him, and she puts her hand on his shoulder. She tells him: "You did well, darling." But Anne is nervous. Facing the police, she looks guilty. She is trying to find something to confess, some sin she committed long ago, for which they want to punish her. She has always been like this, innocent and paranoid. She has never gone through a security check without sweating. One day, sober and pregnant, she blew into a breathalyzer test, convinced that she was about to be arrested.

The captain, a pretty woman with thick brown hair tied back in a ponytail, is sitting on her desk, facing them. She asks Anne how she came into contact with Louise and the reasons she chose to hire her as her children's nanny. Anne replies calmly. All she wants is to satisfy the policewoman, to help her with her enquiries, and—most of all—to find out what Louise is accused of.

Louise was recommended to her by a friend, who spoke very highly of her. And, for that matter, she herself was always satisfied with her nanny. "Hector, as you can tell, was very attached to her."

The captain smiles at the teenage boy. She goes back behind her desk, opens a file and asks: "Do you remember the phone call you got from Mrs. Massé? Just over a year ago, in January?"

"Mrs. Massé?"

"Yes, try to remember. Louise gave you as a reference and Myriam Massé wanted to know what you thought of her."

"That's right, I remember now. I told her that Louise was an exceptional nanny."

They have been sitting for more than two hours in this cold, featureless room. The desk is very neat. There are no photographs on it. There are no wanted posters on the wall. Occasionally the captain stops in the middle of a sentence, apologizes and leaves the office. Anne and her son see her through the window, talking on her mobile phone, whispering in a colleague's ear or drinking a coffee. They have no desire to speak to each other, not even to relieve the boredom. Sitting side by side, they avoid each other, pretending that they have forgotten they are not alone. Sometimes they sigh or stand up and walk around a bit. Hector checks his phone. Anne cradles her black leather handbag. They are bored stiff, but they are too polite and too fearful to show any sign of irritation to the policewoman. Exhausted, submissive, they wait to be released.

The captain prints some documents and hands them to mother and son.

"Sign here and here, please."

Anne bends over the sheet of paper and, without looking up, she asks in a hollow voice: "What did she do? Louise, I mean. What happened?"

"She is accused of killing two children."

There are dark rings around the captain's eyes. Swollen, purplish bags that give her a solemn look and, oddly, make her even prettier.

Hector walks out into the street, into the June heat. The girls are beautiful and he wants to grow up, to be free, to be a man. His eighteen years weigh heavily on him; he'd like to leave them behind, like he left his mother at the door of the police station, dazed and numb. He realizes that what he first felt earlier, when the policewoman told them, was not shock or surprise but an immense and painful relief. A feeling of jubilation, even. As if he'd always known that some menace had hung over him, a pale, sulfurous, unspeakable menace. A menace that he alone, with his child's eyes and heart, was capable of perceiving. Fate had decreed that the calamity would strike elsewhere.

The captain had seemed to understand him. Earlier she had examined his impassive face and she had smiled at him. The way you smile at survivors.

All night long Myriam thinks about that carcass on the kitchen table. As soon as she shuts her eyes, she imagines the animal's skeleton, right there, next to her, in her bed.

She gulped down her wine, one hand on the little table, watching the carcass from the corner of her eye. She was revolted by the idea of touching it. She had the strange feeling that something might happen if she did, that the creature might come back to life and jump at her face, cling to her hair, push her against the wall. She smoked a cigarette by the living-room window and went back into the kitchen. She put on a pair of plastic gloves and threw the skeleton in the trash. She also threw away the plate and the tea towel that had been lying next to it. She hurried downstairs with the black bags and banged the building's front door behind her when she came back in.

She goes to bed. Her heart is pounding so hard in her chest that she finds it hard to breathe. She tries to sleep and then, unable to bear it any longer, she calls Paul and in tears tells him this story of the chicken. He thinks she's overreacting. It's like the script of a bad horror film, he laughs. "Surely you're not going to get into a state like this because of a chicken?" He tries to make her laugh, to make her question the gravity of the situation. Myriam hangs up on him. He tries to call her back but she doesn't answer.

Her insomnia is haunted by accusatory thoughts and then by guilty thoughts. She starts by hurling abuse at Louise. Then she thinks that the nanny must be mad. Maybe dangerous. That she nurses a sordid hatred for her employers, an appetite for vengeance. Myriam blames herself for not having guessed at the violence of which Louise is capable. She had already noticed that the nanny gets angry about this kind of thing. Once, Mila lost a cardigan at school and Louise threw a fit about it. Every day she talked to Myriam about that blue cardigan. She swore she would find it; she harassed the teacher, the caretaker, the dinner ladies. One Monday morning she saw Myriam dressing Mila. The little girl was wearing the blue cardigan.

"You found it?" the nanny asked, looking ecstatic.

"No, but I bought another one."

Louise became uncontrollably angry. "I can't believe I tried so desperately to find it. And what does that mean? You get robbed, you don't take care of your things, but it doesn't matter because Mama will buy Mila a new cardigan?"

And then Myriam turns these accusations against herself. It's my fault, she thinks. I went too far. It was her way of telling me that I was wasteful, frivolous, casual.

Louise must have been offended that I threw away that chicken, when I know that she has money problems. Instead of helping her, I humiliated her.

She gets up at dawn, feeling as if she's hardly slept. When she gets out of bed, she immediately sees that the kitchen light is on. She comes out of her bedroom and sees Louise, sitting in front of the little window that overlooks the courtyard. The nanny is holding her cup of tea—the cup that Myriam bought her for her birthday—in both hands. Her face floats in a cloud of steam. Louise looks like a little old lady, like a ghost trembling in the pale morning. Her hair and her skin are drained of all color. Myriam has the impression that Louise always wears the same clothes nowadays. She feels suddenly sickened by that blue blouse with its Peter Pan collar. She wishes she didn't have to speak to her. She wishes she could make her disappear from her life, with no effort, with a snap of the fingers or a blink of the eyes. But Louise is there; she smiles at her.

In her thin voice, she asks: "Shall I make you a coffee? You look tired."

Myriam reaches out and takes the hot cup.

She thinks about the long day that awaits her; she has to defend a man in court. In her kitchen, face-to-face with Louise, she considers the irony of the situation. She, Myriam Massé—whose pugnacity everyone admires; whose courage when confronting her adversaries Pascal always praises—is terrified by this little blonde woman.

Some teenagers dream of movie sets, football pitches, concert halls packed with fans. Myriam always dreamed of courtrooms. Even as a student, she tried to go as often as she could to watch trials. Her mother didn't understand how anyone could be so passionate about sordid accounts of rapes, about precise, deadpan descriptions of seedy murders or cases of incest. Myriam was preparing for the Bar exam when the trial of the serial killer Michel Fourniret began. She followed the case closely. She'd rented a room in the center of Charleville-Mézières and every day she would join the group of housewives who had come to observe the monster. Outside the courthouse an immense tent had been put up, where the crowd could watch the trial broadcast live on a giant screen. She stood slightly apart from the others. She didn't speak to them. She felt uneasy when these red-faced, short-haired women with their close-cut fingernails would greet the van containing the accused with screamed insults and gobs of spit. Myriam, so full of her principles, so rigid sometimes, was fascinated by that spectacle of open hate, by those calls for vengeance.

Myriam takes the metro and reaches the courthouse early. She smokes a cigarette, her fingertips holding the red string that encircles her huge dossier. For more than a month Myriam has been helping Pascal prepare for this trial. The defendant, a twenty-four-year-old man, is accused of committing a hate crime—along with three accomplices—on two Sri Lankan men. Under the influence of alcohol and cocaine, they beat up the two illegal immigrants, who were employed as cooks. They hit them again and again, hit them until one of the men died, hit them until they realized they had got the wrong men; that they had got their darkies mixed up. They weren't able to explain why. They weren't able to deny the charge either, as they'd been caught in the act by surveillance cameras.

During the first meeting, the man told his lawyers his life story, an account littered with obvious lies and exaggerations. On the threshold of life imprisonment, he tried to charm Myriam. She did all she could to keep a "good distance." That was the expression that Pascal always used; the basis, he said, of a successful case. She sought to disentangle truth from falsehood, methodically, with the evidence to back her up. In her teacher's voice, choosing simple but sharp words, she explained that lying was a poor defense technique and that he had nothing to lose now by telling the truth.

For the trial, she bought the young man a new shirt and advised him not to tell his sick jokes, and to wipe that smug smirk off his face. "We have to prove that you, too, are a victim."

Myriam manages to concentrate, and the work allows her to forget her night of horror. She questions the two experts who stand in the dock to talk about her client's psychological profile. One of the victims gives evidence, with the aid of a translator. The testimony is laborious but the public's emotion is palpable. The accused keeps his eyes lowered, his face impassive.

During a pause in proceedings, while Pascal is on the telephone, Myriam sits in a corridor, staring into space, seized with a sudden panic. She was probably too high-handed in the way she dealt with that issue of Louise's debts. Out of discretion or indifference, she didn't look at the letter from the tax office in much detail. She should have kept the documents, she thinks. Dozens of times she asked Louise to bring them to her. To start with, Louise said she had forgotten them, that she'd think about it tomorrow, she promised. Myriam tried to find out more. She questioned her about Jacques, about those debts that seemed to go back years. She asked her if Stéphanie was aware of her difficulties. But these questions, asked in a gentle, understanding voice, elicited nothing from Louise but an impenetrable silence. It's modesty, Myriam thought. A way of maintaining the frontier between our two worlds. So she gave up trying to help her. She had the awful feeling that her questions were like the lashes of a whip on Louise's fragile body, that body which for the previous few days had seemed to be turning pale, withering, fading away. In this dark corridor, filled by a nagging murmur of voices, Myriam feels bereft, prey to a deep and heavy exhaustion.

This morning Paul called her back. He was gentle and conciliatory. He apologized for having reacted so stupidly. For not having taken her seriously. "We'll do what you want," he told her. "In these circumstances, we can't keep her." And, pragmatic, he added: "We'll wait for the summer. We'll go on vacation, and when we get back we'll make it clear to her that we don't really need her anymore."

Myriam replied in a hollow voice, without conviction. She thinks again of how thrilled the children were when they saw the nanny again after she had been ill for a few days. Of the sad look that Louise had given her. Of her moonlike face. She hears again her hazy and slightly ludicrous excuses, her shame at having failed in her duty. "It won't happen again," she said. "I promise."

Of course, all she has to do is put an end to it. But Louise has the keys to their apartment; she knows everything; she has embedded herself so deeply in their lives that it now seems impossible to remove her. They will drive her away and she'll come back. They'll say their good-byes and she'll knock at the door, she'll come in anyway; she'll threaten them, like a wounded lover.

STÉPHANIE

Stéphanie was very lucky. When she started secondary school, Mrs. Perrin—Louise's employer—offered to enroll the young girl in a Parisian school, one with a much better reputation than the school in Bobigny she was due to attend. The woman had wanted to do a good deed for poor Louise, who worked so hard and was so deserving.

But Stéphanie did not repay this act of generosity. The troubles began only a few weeks after the start of the school year. She disturbed the class. She couldn't stop laughing, throwing objects across the classroom, swearing at her teachers. The other pupils found her simultaneously funny and tiresome. She hid from Louise the notes in her parent-teacher contact book, the warnings, the meetings with the headmaster. She started bunking off and smoking joints in the morning, lying on a bench in a little park in the fifteenth arrondissement.

One evening Mrs. Perrin summoned the nanny to tell her how disappointed she was. She felt betrayed. Because of Louise, she had been humiliated. She had lost face with the headmaster, whom she had spent so long persuading and who had been doing her a favor by accepting Stéphanie. A week later Stéphanie was summoned to the disciplinary council, which Louise was also expected to attend. "It's like a court," her boss explained coldly. "You will have to defend her."

At 3 p.m., Louise and her daughter entered a round, poorly heated room with large windows made of green and blue glass that spread a churchlike light. A dozen people— teachers, counselors, parent-teacher representatives— were sitting around a large wooden table. They all spoke in turn. "Stéphanie is a misfit, undisciplined and rude." "She's not a bad girl," someone added. "But once she gets started, there's no reasoning with her." They are surprised that Louise never reacted, given the scale of this problem. That she didn't respond to the teachers' requests for meetings. They had called her on her mobile. They had even left messages, but she never called them back.

Louise begged them to give her daughter another chance. She explained, in tears, how well she took care of her children; how she punished them when they didn't listen. How she didn't allow them to watch television while doing their homework. She said she had strong principles and a great deal of experience in the education of children. Mrs. Perrin had warned her: this was a trial, and she was the one being judged. Her, the bad mother.

Around the large wooden table, in this freezing room where they all kept their coats on, the teachers tilted their heads sideways. They repeated: "We are not questioning your efforts, madam. We are certain that you are doing your best."

A French teacher—a slim, gentle woman—asked her: "How many brothers and sisters does Stéphanie have?"

"She doesn't have any," replied Louise.

"But you were talking about your children, weren't you?"

"Yes, the children I look after. The ones who stay with me every day. And believe me, my boss is very pleased with the education that I give her children."

They asked her to leave the room so they could deliberate. Louise stood up and smiled at them in a way that she imagined made her look like a woman of the world. In the school corridor, opposite the basketball court, Stéphanie kept laughing idiotically. She was too fat, too tall, and she looked ridiculous with that ponytail on the top of her head. She was wearing printed leggings that made her thighs look enormous. She did not seem intimidated by the formal nature of this meeting, merely bored. She wasn't afraid; on the contrary, she kept smiling knowingly, as if these teachers in their nerdy mohair sweaters and their old-lady scarves were just bad actors.

As soon as she left the meeting room, her good mood returned, along with her dunce's swagger. In the corridor she collared some friends who were coming out of class. She jumped up and down and whispered secrets in the ear of a shy girl who suppressed a laugh. Louise wanted to slap her, to shake her as violently as she could. She wished she could make her understand how humiliating and exhausting it was bringing up a daughter like her. She wished she could rub Stéphanie's nose in her sweat and her anxieties, could wipe that stupid, carefree smile off her face. She wanted to rip apart what remained of her childhood.

In that noisy corridor, Louise forced herself not to tremble. She gradually reduced Stéphanie to silence by tightening her fingers' grip around her daughter's chubby arm.

"You can come back in."

The headmaster poked his head through the doorway and beckoned them to return to their seats. The deliberation had taken only ten minutes, but Louise didn't realize that was a bad sign.

Once the mother and daughter had sat down again, the headmaster began to speak. Stéphanie, he explained, was a disruptive element that all of them had tried and failed to control. They had used every educational method they knew, but nothing had worked. They had exhausted every possibility. They had a responsibility and they simply could not allow her to take an entire class hostage. "Perhaps," he added, "Stéphanie would be more comfortable in a neighborhood closer to home. In an environment more suited to her, where she would have more points of reference. You understand?"

This was March. It still felt like winter. It seemed as if the cold weather would never end. "If you need help with the administrative aspects, there are people for that," the career adviser reassured her. Louise did not understand. Stéphanie was expelled.

On the bus home, Louise stayed silent. Stéphanie

giggled; she looked through the window, earbuds stuck in her ears. They walked up the gray street that led to Jacques's house. They passed the market and Stéphanie slowed down to look at the stalls. Louise felt a surge of hate for her; for her offhand reaction, her adolescent self-ishness. She grabbed her by the sleeve and dragged her away with incredible strength and abruptness. Anger filled her, an anger that grew ever darker and more heated. She wanted to dig her nails into her daughter's soft skin.

She opened the small front door. Barely had she closed it behind them than she started showering Stéphanie with blows. She hit her on the back to start with, heavy punches that threw her daughter to the floor. The teenager curled up in a ball and cried out. Louise kept hitting her. She summoned all her colossal strength. Again and again her tiny hands slapped Stéphanie's face. She tore her hair and pulled apart the girl's arms, uncovering her head. She hit her in the eyes. She insulted her. She scratched her until she bled. When Stéphanie didn't move anymore, Louise spat in her face.

Jacques heard the noise and he went up to the window. He watched Louise punishing her daughter but made no attempt to separate them.

The silences and misunderstandings have infected everything. In the apartment, the atmosphere grows heavier. Myriam tries not to let the children perceive it, but she is more distant with Louise. She speaks to her in a clipped voice, giving her precise instructions. She follows Paul's advice, which she repeats to herself: "She's our employee, not our friend."

They no longer drink tea together in the kitchen, Myriam sitting at the table and Louise leaning on the countertop. Myriam no longer pays her compliments: "Louise, you're an angel" or "You're the best nanny in the world." She no longer offers, on Friday nights, to share a bottle of rosé, forgotten at the back of the fridge. "The children are watching a video. Why don't we have some fun too?" Myriam used to say. Now, when one of them opens the door, the other closes it behind her. They are hardly ever in the same room anymore, the two of them avoiding each other's presence in a perfectly synced choreography.

Then spring comes, dazzling and sudden. The days grow longer and the first buds brighten the trees. The good weather sweeps away their winter habits; Louise takes the children outside, to parks. One evening she asks Myriam if she can finish earlier. "I have a date," she explains, her voice trembling slightly.

She meets Hervé in the neighborhood where he works. Together they go to the cinema. Hervé would rather have gone for a drink on the terrace of a café, but Louise insisted. And she likes the film so much that they go back to see it again the following week. Next to her in the darkness, Hervé dozes discreetly.

In the end she agrees to have a drink with him on a terrace, outside a bar on one of the Grands Boulevards. Hervé is a happy man, she thinks. He smiles as he talks about his plans. The vacations they could take together in the Vosges. They would go skinny-dipping in the lakes; they would sleep in a mountain chalet belonging to a man he knows. And they would listen to music all the time. He would play her his record collection and he is sure that, very soon, she wouldn't be able to live without music. Hervé is ready to retire and he can't imagine enjoying those years of rest and relaxation on his own. His marriage ended in divorce fifteen years ago. He has no children and solitude weighs heavily on him.

Hervé tried every ploy in the book before Louise finally agreed, one evening, to go home with him. He waits for her at the Paradis, the café opposite the Massés' apartment building. They take the metro together and Hervé puts his red-skinned hand on Louise's knee. As she listens to him, her eyes are fixed on that hand, that man's hand which settles, starts to move, wants more. That discreet hand which tries to hide its intentions.

They make love clumsily, him on top of her, their chins sometimes banging together. Lying on her, he grunts, but she doesn't know if it's a grunt of pleasure or because his joints are hurting and she's not helping him. Hervé is so short that she can feel his ankles against hers—his thick ankles, his hairy feet—and, to her, this contact seems more incongruous, more intrusive than the man's sex organ inside her. Jacques was so tall and he made love like he was punishing her, angrily. After this embrace, Hervé emerges relieved, as if a heavy weight has been lifted from him, and he acts more familiarly toward her.

It was here, in Hervé's bed, in his council house in the Porte de Saint-Ouen, with the man asleep beside her, that she thought about a baby. A tiny baby, just born, a baby completely enveloped in that warm smell of life just beginning. A baby abandoned to love, which she would dress in pastel-colored romper suits and which would be passed from her arms to Myriam's and then to Paul's. A newborn that would bind them more closely to one another, bringing them together in the same surge of tenderness. That would erase all the misunderstandings, the dissensions, that would give meaning to their daily habits. She would rock this baby on her knees for hours in a little room, illuminated only by a nightlight that would project boats and islands on to the wall. She would caress its bald head and gently insert her little finger into its mouth. The child would stop crying then, sucking her polished fingernail with its swollen gums.

The next day she makes Paul and Myriam's bed more carefully than usual. She moves her hand over the sheets. She searches for a trace of their lovemaking, a trace of the child she is now sure is going to arrive. She asks Mila if she would like a little brother or a little sister. "A baby we could look after together—what do you think?" Louise hopes that Mila will talk about this to her mother, that she will whisper this idea into her ear and from there it will enter her mind and grow stronger. And one day the little girl asks Myriam, under Louise's delighted gaze, if she has a baby in her belly. "Oh, God, no, I'd rather die!" Myriam laughs.

Louise thinks that is bad. She doesn't understand Myriam's laughter, the lighthearted way she answers this question. Myriam is saying that, she thinks, to ward off bad luck. She feigns indifference, but she thinks about it all the same. In September, Adam too will start school; the house will be empty, and Louise will have nothing to do. Another child has to arrive to fill the long winter days.

Louise listens to conversations. It's a small apartment— she isn't doing it deliberately—but she ends up knowing everything. Except that, recently, Myriam has been speaking more quietly. She closes the door behind her when she talks on the phone. She whispers, her lips just above Paul's shoulder. They look as if they are keeping secrets.

Louise talks to Wafa about this child that will soon be born. About the joy it will bring, and the extra work. "With three children, they won't be able to do without me." Louise has moments of euphoria. She has the vague, fleeting sense of a life that will grow bigger, of wider open spaces, a purer love, voracious appetites. She thinks about the summer, which is so close, and their family vacations. She imagines the smell of plowed soil and olive pits rotting by a roadside. The vault of fruit trees under a moonbeam and nothing to carry, nothing to cover up, nothing to hide.

She starts cooking properly again; in the past few weeks her meals have become almost inedible. For Myriam, she makes cinnamon rice pudding, spicy soups and all sorts of dishes reputed to increase fertility. She observes the young woman's body as attentively as a jealous husband. She examines the fairness of her complexion, the weight of her breasts, the shine of her hair: all, she believes, signs of pregnancy.

She takes care of the laundry with the concentration of a witch, a voodoo priestess. As always, she empties the washing machine. She stretches Paul's boxer shorts. She washes Myriam's lingerie by hand; in the kitchen sink, she runs cold water over the lace and silk of her bras and knickers. She recites prayers.

But Louise is always disappointed. She doesn't need to rip open the trash bags. Nothing escapes her. She saw the stain on the pajama bottoms left by Myriam's side of the bed. On the bathroom floor this morning, she noticed the tiny drop of blood. A drop so small that Myriam didn't clean it, and which was left to dry on the green-and-white tiles.

The blood returns ceaselessly; she knows its odor, this blood that Myriam cannot hide from her and that, each month, announces the death of a child.

Euphoria gives way to days of dejection. The world seems to shrink, to retract, to weigh down on her body, to crush it. Paul and Myriam close doors on her and she wants to smash them down. She has only one desire: to create a world with them, to find her place and live there, to dig herself a niche, a burrow, a warm hiding place. Sometimes she feels ready to claim her portion of earth and then the urge wanes, she is overcome by sorrow, and she feels ashamed even to have believed in something.

One Thursday evening, around 8 p.m., Louise goes back to her studio flat. The landlord is waiting in the dark corridor. He stands beneath the bulb that no longer works. "Ah, there you are." Bertrand Alizard practically pounces on her. He aims the light from his phone screen at Louise's face and she covers her eyes with her hands. "I was waiting for you. I've come here several times, in the evenings and afternoons. I never found you." He speaks smoothly, his upper body leaning toward Louise, as if he is about to touch her, take her arm, whisper in her ear. He stares at her with his gummed-up eyes, his lashless eyes that he rubs after taking off his glasses, which are attached to a string around his neck.

She opens the door to her flat and lets him in. Bertrand Alizard is wearing a pair of beige trousers that are too big for him. Observing him from behind, Louise notices that the belt has missed two loops and that his trousers hang loose at his waist and beneath his backside. He looks like an old man, stooped and frail, who has stolen a giant's clothing. Everything about him seems harmless: his balding head, his wrinkled cheeks covered in freckles, his trembling shoulders . . . everything except his huge, dry hands, with their thick nails like fossils; his butcher's hands, which he rubs together to warm up.

He enters the apartment in silence, slowly and carefully, as if he were discovering the place for the first time. He inspects the walls, runs his finger over the spotless skirting boards. He touches everything with his calloused hands, caresses the sofa's slipcover, strokes the surface of the Formica table. To him, the apartment appears empty, uninhabited. He would have liked to make a few remarks to his tenant, to tell her that in addition to paying her rent late, she is failing to take care of the flat. But the room is exactly as it was when he left it to her, the day she visited the studio for the first time.

He stands with one hand on the back of a chair and looks at Louise. He waits, staring at her with his yellow eyes that don't see much anymore but that he is not ready to lower. He waits for her to speak, or to rummage in her handbag for the rent money she owes. He waits for her to make the first move, to apologize for not having replied to his letters or the messages he left on her phone. But Louise doesn't say a word. She remains standing against the door, like one of those little dogs that bite you when you try to calm them down.

"You've started packing up, by the looks of it. That's good." Alizard points, with his thick finger, at a few boxes in the entrance hall. "The next tenant will be here in a month."

He takes a few steps and tentatively pushes open the door of the shower cubicle. The porcelain bowl has sunk into the ground, and the rotten planks beneath it have given way.

"What happened here?"

The landlord squats down. He mutters to himself, takes off his jacket and drops it on the floor, then puts on his glasses. Louise stands behind him.

Mr. Alizard turns around and says in a louder voice: "I asked you what happened!"

Louise jumps. "I don't know. It happened a few days ago. The shower's old, I think."

"No, it's not! I built this shower cubicle myself. You should think yourself lucky. Before, people used to wash in the bathroom on the landing. It was me, on my own, who put the shower in this studio."

"It collapsed."

"You didn't look after it, obviously. Surely you don't think I'm going to pay for this to be repaired when you're the one who let it rot?"

Louise stares at him and Mr. Alizard cannot guess what that closed, silent look means.

"Why didn't you call me? How long have you been living like this?" Mr. Alizard squats down again, his forehead covered in sweat.

Louise does not tell him that this studio is merely a lair, a parenthesis where she comes to hide her exhaustion. That she lives somewhere else. Every day she takes a shower in Myriam and Paul's apartment. She undresses in their bedroom and delicately places her clothes on the couple's bed. Then, naked, she crosses the living room to reach the bathroom. Adam sits on the floor and she walks past him. She looks at the babbling child and she knows he will not betray her secret. He will not say anything about Louise's body, its marble whiteness, her mother-of-pearl breasts, which have seen so little sunlight.

She leaves the bathroom door open so she can hear him. She turns on the water and for a long time—as long as possible—she remains motionless under the burning jet. She doesn't get dressed again straight away. She sinks her fingers into the pots of cream that Myriam hordes and she massages her calves, her thighs, her arms. She walks barefoot through the apartment, her body wrapped in a white towel. Her own towel, which she hides every day under a pile in a cupboard.

"You noticed the problem and you didn't try to fix it? You'd rather live like a gypsy?"

Crouching in front of the shower, Alizard hams it up. This studio in the suburbs, he only kept it out of sentimentality. He exhales loudly and puts his hands to his forehead. He touches the black foam with his fingertips and shakes his head, as if only he could possibly understand the gravity of the situation. Out loud, he calculates the cost of the repair work. "That's going to cost about eight hundred euros. At least." He dazzles her with the science of DIY, using technical words, claiming that it will take him more than two weeks to repair this disaster. He tries to impress the little blonde woman, who still says nothing.

She can pay for it out of her deposit, he thinks. When she moved in, he insisted that she pay him two months' rent in advance, as a form of security. It's sad, but the truth is you can't trust people. As far as the landlord can remember, he has never had to pay back that sum to any of his tenants. Nobody is careful enough: there is always something to be found, a defect to be highlighted, a stain somewhere, a scratch.

Alizard has a head for business. For thirty years he drove a lorry between France and Poland. He slept in his cab, barely ate, lied about his rest time, resisted every temptation. He consoled himself for all of this by calculating the money he'd saved. He felt pleased with himself, proud of his ability to make such sacrifices in preparation for his future fortune.

Year after year he bought studio flats in the Paris suburbs and renovated them. He rents them out, at an exorbitant price, to people who have no alternative. At the end of each month he goes around to all of his properties to pick up his rent. He pokes his head through doorways; sometimes he goes inside, to "have a look around," to "make sure everything's in order." He asks indiscreet questions, to which the tenants reply grudgingly, desperate for him to leave, to get out of their kitchen, to take his nose out of their cupboard. But he stays there and in the end they offer him something to drink, which he accepts and slowly sips. He tells them about his backache ("Thirty years driving a lorry, it messes you up"). He makes conversation.

He likes to rent to women, because they're more conscientious and less likely to cause trouble. He particularly favors students, single mothers, divorcees—but not old women, who can move in and stop paying and still have the law on their side. And then Louise arrived, with her sad smile, her blonde hair, her lost-waif expression. She was recommended by one of Alizard's former tenants, a nurse at the Henri-Mondor hospital who had always paid her rent on time.

Bloody sentimentality. This Louise had nobody. No children and a dead husband. She stood there in front of him, a wad of euros in her hand, and he thought she was pretty, elegant in her blouse with its Peter Pan collar. She looked at him, docile and grateful. She whispered: "I was very ill," and in that moment he was eager to ask her questions, to ask her what she'd done after her husband's death, where she had come from and what pain she had suffered. But she didn't give him time. She said: "I've just found a job, in Paris, with a very good family." And the conversation ended there.

Now Bertrand Alizard wants to get rid of this mute, negligent tenant. He's no longer fooled. He won't put up with any more of her excuses, her shifty behavior, her late payments. He doesn't know why, but the sight of Louise makes him shiver. Something in her disgusts him: that enigmatic smile, that excessive makeup; that way she has of looking down on him, her mouth tight-lipped. Not once has she ever responded to one of his smiles. Not once has she made the effort to notice that he's wearing a new jacket and that he's brushed his sad few strands of red hair to the side.

Alizard heads over to the sink. He washes his hands and says: "I'll come back in a week with the parts and a plumber to do the work. You should finish packing."

Louise takes the children for walks. They spend long afternoons in the park, where the trees have been pruned, where the lawn—green once again—attracts the local students. Around the swings, the children are happy to see one another again, even if they don't know anyone's names. For them, nothing else matters but this latest fancy-dress costume, this new toy, this miniature stroller in which a little girl has nestled her baby.

Louise has only one friend in the neighborhood. Apart from Wafa, she speaks with nobody. She offers nothing more than polite smiles, discreet waves. When she first arrived, the other nannies in the park kept their distance. Louise was like a chaperone, a quartermaster, an English governess. The others disliked her haughty airs, her ludicrous *grande dame* pose. There was something sanctimonious about the way she didn't have the decency to look away when another nanny, phone glued to her ear, forgot to hold a child's hand as they crossed the road. Sometimes she would even make a point of telling off unsupervised children who stole toys from others or fell off a guardrail.

As the months passed, the nannies—sitting on those benches for hours on end—gradually got to know one another, almost despite themselves, as if they were coworkers sharing an open-air office. Every day after school they would see one another, in the supermarket, at the doctor's or by the merry-go-round in the little square. Louise remembers some of their names and countries of origin. She knows the apartment buildings where they work, their bosses' occupations. Sitting under the barely flowering rose bush, she listens to the interminable conversations that these women have on their phones as they nibble chocolate biscuits.

Around the slide and the sandpit she hears snatches of Baoulé, Dyula, Arabic and Hindi, sweet nothings whispered in Filipino or Russian. Languages from all over the world contaminate the babbling of the children, who learn odd words and repeat them to their enchanted parents. "He speaks Arabic, I swear! Listen to him." Then, with the passing years, the children forget. And as the face and the voice of the now-vanished nanny fade from memory, nobody in the house recalls how to say "Mama" in Lingala or the name of the exotic dishes that the nice nanny used to make. "That meat stew, what did she call it again?"

Around the children—who all look alike, often wearing the same clothes bought in the same shops, with their names written on the labels by their mothers to avoid any confusion—buzzes this swarm of women. There are young women in black veils, who have to be even gentler, cleaner and more punctual than the others. There are the ones who change wigs every week. The Filipinos who beg the children, in English, not to jump in puddles. There are the old ones, who have worked in the neighborhood for years, who are on familiar terms with the school headmistress; the ones who see teenagers in the streets who they used to look after when they were little and persuade themselves that the teenager recognized them, that he would have said hello if he wasn't so shy. There are the new ones, who work for a few months and then vanish without saying good-bye, leaving trails of rumors and suspicions behind them.

About Louise, the nannies know very little. Even Wafa, who seems pretty close to her, has been discreet about her friend's life. They have tried asking her questions. The white nanny intrigues them. How many times have the other parents used her as a benchmark, vaunting her qualities as a cook, her total availability, mentioning the complete trust Myriam puts in her? They wonder who she is, this fragile, perfect woman. Who did she work for before she came here? In which part of Paris? Is she married? Does she have children who she picks up in the evening, after work? Are her bosses good to her?

Louise does not respond—or hardly—and the nannies understand this silence. They all have shameful secrets. They hide awful memories of bent knees, humiliations, lies. Memories of barely audible voices on the other end of the line, of conversations cut off, of people who die and are never seen again, of money needed day after day for a sick child who no longer recognizes you and who has forgotten the sound of your voice. Some of them, Louise knows, have stolen—just little things, almost nothing at all—like a tax levied on the happiness of others. Some conceal their real names. It never even crosses their minds to blame Louise for her reserve. They are wary, that's all.

In the park, they don't talk much about themselves, or only by allusion. They don't want the tears to well in their eyes. Their bosses are fodder enough for animated conversations. The nannies laugh at their obsessions, their habits, their way of life. Wafa's bosses are stingy; Alba's are horribly suspicious. The mother of little Jules has a drinking problem. Most of them, the nannies complain, are manipulated by their children; they see very little of them and constantly give in to their demands. Rosalia, a very dark-skinned Filipino woman, chain-smokes cigarettes. "The boss surprised me in the street last time. I know she's spying on me."

While the children run around on the gravel, while they dig in the sandpit (the rats that lived there having recently been exterminated by the local authorities), the women turn the park into a cross between a recruitment office, a union headquarters, a claims center and a classified-ads listing. Here there is talk of job offers and disputes between employers and employees. The women come to complain to Lydie, the self-proclaimed president, a tall woman in her fifties from the Ivory Coast who wears fake-fur coats and has thin red-pencil eyebrows.

At 6 p.m., groups of youths invade the park. The nannies know them. They're from the Rue de Dunkerque, from the Gare du Nord. The nannies know that these youths leave broken crack pipes by the edge of the playground, that they piss in flowerbeds, go looking for fights. Seeing them, the nannies quickly pick up children's coats and toy excavators covered in sand, they hang their handbags from the handles of the strollers, and they leave.

The procession goes through the park's gates and the women go their separate ways: some walk up toward Montmartre or Notre-Dame-de-Lorette; others, like Louise and Lydie, head down toward the Grands Boulevards. They walk side by side. Louise holds hands with Mila and Adam. When the sidewalk is narrow, she lets Lydie walk ahead of them, bent over her stroller with a baby asleep inside it.

"A young pregnant woman came by yesterday. She's going to have twins in August," Lydie tells her.

Everyone knows that some mothers—the most sensible and conscientious ones—come here nanny-shopping, the way people used to go down to the docks or to the end of an alley to find a maid or a warehouseman. The mothers prowl around the benches, observing the nannies, examining the faces of the children when they go running to the thighs of these women, who brusquely blow their nose or console them after a fall. Sometimes the mothers ask questions. They investigate.

"She lives on Rue des Martyrs and she's due at the end of August. She's looking for someone, so I thought of you," Lydie concludes.

Louise looks up at her with her doll-like eyes. She hears Lydie's voice, as if from far away; the sound echoes inside her head but the words are a blur and she doesn't grasp their meaning. She leans down, takes Adam in her arms and puts her hand under Mila's armpit. Lydie raises her voice; she repeats something. She thinks that perhaps

Louise didn't hear her, that she's distracted, her mind wholly occupied by the children.

"So what do you think? Shall I give her your number?"

Louise does not reply. She gathers speed and pushes past, brutal, silent. She cuts in front of Lydie and as she makes her escape, she knocks over the stroller with a sudden gesture, waking the baby, which starts to scream.

"What the hell is wrong with you?" shouts the nanny as all her shopping falls into the gutter. Louise is already far away. In the street, people gather around Lydie. They pick up mandarins that have rolled along the sidewalk; they throw the soaked baguette in a trash can. They worry about the baby, who is fine, thankfully.

Lydie will recount this incredible story several times, and each time she will swear: "No, it wasn't an accident. She knocked over the stroller on purpose."

Her obsession with the child spins endlessly in her mind. She thinks of nothing else. This baby, which she will love madly, is the solution to all her problems. Once it's on its way, it will shut up the harpies in the park, it will drive away her horrible landlord. It will protect Louise's place in her kingdom. She feels sure that Paul and Myriam don't have enough time to themselves. That Mila and Adam are an obstacle to the baby's arrival. It's the children's fault if their parents are never alone together. Paul and Myriam are exhausted by their tantrums; Adam wakes up too often in the night, cutting short their lovemaking. If the children weren't constantly under their feet—whining, demanding cuddles—Paul and Myriam would be able to forge ahead and make a child for Louise. Her desire for that baby is fanatical, violent, blindly possessive. She wants it in a way she has rarely wanted anything: so badly it hurts, to the point where she is capable of choking, burning, destroying anything that comes between her and the satisfaction of her desire.

One evening, Louise waits impatiently for Myriam.

When her boss finally opens the door, Louise practically jumps on her, eyes ablaze. She is holding Mila by the hand. The nanny appears tense, concentrated. She looks as if she's making a great effort to contain herself, not to hop up and down or yell something. She has been thinking about this moment all day long. Her plan seems perfect to her, and now all she needs is for Myriam to agree, to let her do it, and to fall into Paul's arms.

"I'd like to take the children to eat at a restaurant. That way, you'll be able to have a nice dinner with your husband."

Myriam puts her handbag on the chair. Louise watches her; she moves closer, stands next to her. Myriam can feel the nanny's breath on her; her presence makes it impossible for Myriam to think. Louise is like a child whose eyes are saying "So?," whose entire body is stiff with impatience, exaltation.

"Oh, I don't know. We haven't planned anything. Maybe another time." Myriam takes off her jacket and starts walking to her bedroom. But Mila holds her back. The child enters the scene, following the nanny's script to perfection. In a sweet voice, she begs: "Mama, please. We want to go to a restaurant with Louise."

At last Myriam gives in. She insists on paying for their meal and begins to rummage in her handbag for cash, but Louise stops her. "Don't. Please. Tonight, I want to take them out."

Inside her pocket, against her thigh, Louise holds a banknote, which she caresses sometimes with her fingertips. They walk to the restaurant. She spotted this little bistro a while ago; its customers are mostly students, who come here to drink its three-euro beer. But tonight the bistro is practically empty. The owner, a Chinese man, sits behind the bar, in the neon light. He wears a garishly patterned red shirt and he is chatting with a woman who sits in front of a glass of beer, socks rolled up over her fat ankles. Out on the terrace, two men are smoking.

Louise pushes Mila inside the restaurant. The air is thick with the smell of stale tobacco, meat stew and sweat, and it makes the little girl want to throw up. Mila is very disappointed. She sits down and looks around the empty room, her eyes searching the dirty shelves with pots of ketchup and mustard on them. This is not what she had been imagining. She expected to see pretty ladies; she thought there would be noise, music, lovers. Instead of which, she slumps over the greasy table and stares at the television screen above the bar.

Louise, with Adam in her lap, says she doesn't want to eat. "I'll choose for you, okay?" Without giving Mila time to reply, she orders sausages and chips. "They'll share it," she explains. The Chinese man barely responds. He takes the menu from her hands.

Louise also orders a glass of wine, which she sips very slowly. She tries to make conversation with Mila. She has brought some pencils and sheets of paper, which she puts on the table. But Mila has no desire to draw. She's not very hungry either and hardly touches her meal. Adam has gone back inside his stroller. He rubs his eyes with his little fists.

Louise looks through the window. She looks at her watch, at the street, at the bar where the owner leans his elbows. She bites her nails, smiles, then her eyes turn vague, absent. She would like to find something for her hands to do, focus her mind on one single idea, but her thoughts are like broken glass, her soul weighed down by rocks. Several times, she passes her folded hand over the table, as if to sweep away invisible crumbs or smooth the cold surface. A jumble of unrelated images fills her head; visions that flash past ever faster, connecting memories to regrets, faces to unfulfilled fantasies. The smell of plastic in the hospital courtyard where they took her for walks. The sound of Stéphanie's laughter, at once blaring and muffled, like the noise a hyena makes. The faces of forgotten children; the softness of hair, stroked with her fingertips; the chalky taste of an apple turnover that had dried out at the bottom of a bag, but that she'd eaten anyway. She hears Bertrand Alizard's voice, his lying voice, which mingles with other voices, the voices of all those who gave her instructions, advice, orders; the surprisingly gentle voice of that female bailiff whose name, she remembers, was Isabelle.

Louise smiles at Mila. She wants to console her. She can tell that the little girl is on the verge of tears. She recognizes that feeling, that weight on the chest, that discomfort at being there. She also knows that Mila is restraining herself, that she has self-control, bourgeois manners, that she is capable of a thoughtfulness beyond her age. Louise orders another glass of wine. While she drinks, she watches Mila stare at the television screen, and she can make out, very clearly, her mother's features beneath the mask of childhood. Those innocent, little-girl gestures are the bud containing the woman's edginess, the boss's severity.

The Chinese man picks up the empty glasses and the half-full plate. He puts the bill—scribbled on a scrap of graph paper—on the table. Louise doesn't move. She waits for the time to pass, for the sky outside to grow darker; she thinks about Paul and Myriam, enjoying their time alone, about the empty apartment, the meal she left for them on the table. They've eaten by now, she imagines, standing up in the kitchen, the way they used to do before the children were born. Paul pours his wife more wine and finishes his own glass. His hand slides over Myriam's skin and they laugh. That's the kind of people they are: they laugh with love, with desire, shameless.

At last Louise stands up. They leave the restaurant. Mila is relieved. Her eyelids are heavy; she wants to go to bed now. In his stroller, Adam has fallen asleep. Louise straightens his blanket. As soon as night falls, the winter cold returns from its hiding place, sneaking under their clothes.

Louise holds the little girl's hand, and for a long time they walk through city streets where all the other children have disappeared. In the Grands Boulevards, they pass theaters and packed cafés. They head down streets that become ever darker and narrower, sometimes emerging into a little square where young people lean against trash cans, smoking joints.

Mila does not recognize these streets. A yellow glow illuminates the sidewalks. To her, these houses, these restaurants seem very far from home and she looks up at Louise with anxious eyes. She waits for a reassuring word. A surprise, perhaps? But Louise just keeps walking and walking, breaking her silence only to mutter: "Come on—aren't you coming?" The little girl twists her ankles on the cobblestones. Her stomach is racked with anxiety. She feels sure that, if she complained, it would only make things worse. She senses that a tantrum would do no good. In Rue Montmartre, Mila observes the girls smoking outside bars, the girls in high heels, who shout too loud, causing the bar owner to bark at them: "Shut up, will you? We've got neighbors here." Mila is completely lost; she doesn't know if this is even the same city, if she can see her house from here, if her parents know where she is.

Abruptly, Louise stops in the middle of a busy sidewalk. She glances up, parks the stroller next to a wall and asks Mila: "What flavor do you want?"

Behind the counter a man waits wearily for the child to make up her mind. Mila is too small to see the trays of ice cream, so she stands on tiptoes and then answers nervously: "Strawberry."

One hand holding Louise's, the other gripping her cone, Mila walks back the way they've come through the darkness of the night, licking her ice cream, which gives her a terrible headache. She squeezes her eyes shut to make the pain go away, trying to concentrate on the taste of crushed strawberries and the little pieces of fruit that get stuck between her teeth. Inside her empty stomach, the ice cream falls in heavy flakes.

They take the bus home. Mila asks if she can put the ticket in the machine, as she does whenever they take the bus together. But Louise shushes her. "We don't need a ticket at night. Don't worry about it."

―――――――

When Louise opens the door of the apartment, Paul is lying on the sofa. He is listening to a record, eyes closed. Mila rushes over to him. She jumps in his arms and buries her frozen face in her father's neck. Paul pretends to tell her off for coming home so late, going out and having fun at a restaurant, like a big girl. Myriam, he tells them, took a bath and went to bed early. "She was exhausted by work. I didn't even see her."

A sudden melancholy chokes Louise. So all that was for nothing. She is cold, her legs ache, she spent the last of her cash, and Myriam didn't even wait for her husband before she went to sleep.

She feels alone with the children. Children don't care about the contours of our world. They can guess at its harshness, its darkness, but they don't want to know anything more. Louise tells them about it and they turn away. She holds their hands, crouches down so they are at the same level, but already they are looking elsewhere: they've seen something. They've found a game that gives them an excuse not to hear. They don't pretend to feel sorry for those less fortunate than them.

She sits next to Mila. The little girl is squatting on a chair, drawing pictures. She is capable of staying focused on her sheets of paper and her pile of felt-tip pens for nearly an hour. She colors the picture carefully, attentive to the smallest details. Louise likes to sit next to her, to watch as the colors are spread over the paper. She observes, in silence, the blooming of giant flowers in the garden of an orange house where people with long hands and tall, slender bodies sleep on the lawn. Mila leaves no empty spaces. Clouds, flying cars, hot-air balloons fill the densely shimmering sky.

"Who's that?" Louise asks.

"That?" Mila puts her finger on a huge, smiling figure, lying on the lawn and covering more than half of the page. "That's Mila."

Louise can no longer find any consolation in the children. The stories she tells them get stuck in a rut and Mila points this out to her. The mythical creatures have lost their vivacity, their splendor. Now her characters have forgotten what they are fighting for, and her tales are just descriptions of long, broken, confused wanderings, impoverished princesses, sick dragons; selfish soliloquies that the children don't understand and of which they soon grow weary. "Think of something else," Mila begs her, but Louise can't. She is sinking into her own words as into quicksand.

Louise doesn't laugh as much anymore. She puts less enthusiasm into their pillow fights and games of ludo. And yet she adores these two children, whom she spends hours observing. It's enough to make her cry sometimes, the looks they give her when they want her approval or her help. Most of all, she loves the way Adam looks around at her, wanting her to notice his improvements, his joys, to show her that in everything he does there is something that is meant for her, and her alone. She would like to drink in their innocence, their excitement, until she is intoxicated. She would like to see through their eyes when they look at something for the first time, when they understand the logic of a mechanism, expecting it to repeat itself infinitely without ever thinking of the weariness that will one day slow it down.

All day long Louise leaves the television on. She

watches apocalyptic news reports, idiotic shows, games whose rules she doesn't fully understand. Since the terrorist attacks, Myriam has forbidden her to let the children watch television. But Louise doesn't care. Mila knows she must not tell her parents what she has seen. That she mustn't say the words "hunt," "terrorist," "killed." The child watches the news in rapt silence. Then, when she's had enough, she turns to her brother. They play, they fight. Mila pushes him against the wall and the little boy turns red before retaliating.

Louise does not look around. She stays where she is, eyes glued to the screen, her body completely immobile. The nanny refuses to go to the park. She doesn't want to talk to the other women or see the old neighbor, whom she humiliated herself with by offering her services. The children get cranky and pace around the apartment. They beg her: they want to go outside, to play with their friends, to buy a chocolate waffle at the top of the street.

The children's cries irritate her; she's ready to scream too. The children's nagging whines, their foghorn voices, their "why?"s, their selfish desires seem to split her skull. "When is tomorrow?" Mila asks, hundreds of times. Louise can't sing a song without them begging her to do it again; they want the eternal repetition of everything— stories, games, funny faces—and Louise can't stand it anymore. She has no patience now for their tears, their tantrums, their hysterical excitement. Sometimes she wants to put her fingers around Adam's neck and squeeze until he faints. She shakes her head to get rid of these thoughts. She manages to stop thinking about it, but a dark and slimy tide has completely submerged her.

———————

Someone has to die. Someone has to die for us to be happy.

Morbid refrains echo inside Louise's head when she walks. Phrases that she didn't invent—and whose meaning she is not sure she fully grasps—fill her mind. Her heart has grown hard. The years have covered it in a thick, cold rind and she can barely hear it beating. Nothing moves her anymore. She has to admit that she no longer knows how to love. All the tenderness has been squeezed from her heart. Her hands have nothing left to caress.

I'll be punished for that, she hears herself think. I'll be punished for not knowing how to love.

There are photographs of that afternoon. They have not been printed but they exist, somewhere, deep inside an artificial memory. The pictures are mostly of the children. Adam, half-naked, lying in the grass. He is staring absently to the side, with his big blue eyes, his expression almost melancholic despite his tender age. In one of those images, Mila is running down a broad, tree-lined path. She is wearing a white dress with a butterfly design. She is barefoot. In another photo, Paul is carrying Adam on his shoulders and Mila in his arms. Myriam is behind the lens. Her husband's face is blurred, his smile hidden by one of Adam's little feet. Myriam laughs too; she doesn't think to ask them to keep still. To stop wriggling for a moment. "Please? I'm trying to take a picture."

She is fond of these photographs, though. She takes hundreds of them and looks at them in melancholy moments. In the metro, between two meetings, sometimes even during a meal, she scrolls through portraits of her children. She also believes it is her duty as a mother to immortalize these instants, to possess the proof of past joys.

One day she will be able to show them to Mila or Adam. She will recount her memories and the image will awaken old sensations, details, an atmosphere. She has always been told that children are just an ephemeral happiness, a fleeting vision, a restlessness. An eternal metamorphosis. Round faces that are gradually imbued with seriousness without us even realizing. So, every chance she gets, she looks at her children from behind the screen of her iPhone. For her, those small beings are the most beautiful landscape in the world.

Paul's friend Thomas invited them to spend the day at his country house. He goes there, alone, to write songs and nurse his alcoholism. Thomas keeps ponies at the bottom of his garden. Picture-book ponies, with short legs and hair as blonde as an American actress. A little stream runs through the vast garden, whose borders even Thomas doesn't know. The children eat lunch on the grass. The parents drink rosé and in the end Thomas puts the box of wine on the table and helps himself to glass after glass. "We're among friends, aren't we? Let's just get stuck in."

Thomas has no children, and it doesn't even cross Paul or Myriam's mind to bother him with their worries about the nanny, the kids' education or family vacations. During this beautiful May day, they forget their anxieties. Their preoccupations appear to them as they are: minor everyday concerns, mere vagaries. All they think about now is the future, their plans, their ripening happiness. Myriam is sure that Pascal will ask her to become a partner in September. She will be able to choose her cases, delegate the drudgery to interns. Paul looks at his wife and his children.

He thinks to himself that the hardest work is over, that the best is yet to come.

They spend a glorious day running around and playing. The children ride ponies and feed them apples and carrots. They pull weeds from what Thomas calls the vegetable garden, even though not a single vegetable has ever grown there. Paul grabs a guitar and makes everyone laugh. Then everyone falls silent when Thomas sings and Myriam harmonizes. The children stare wide-eyed at these calm adults singing in a language that they don't understand.

When it's time to go home, the children howl in protest. Adam throws himself on the ground and refuses to leave. Mila, who is also exhausted, sobs in Thomas's arms. Almost as soon as they're inside the car, the children fall asleep. Myriam and Paul are silent. They watch the fields of rapeseed lying stunned in the fawn sunset that paints the motorway rest areas, the industrial zones, the gray wind turbines with a touch of poetry.

The motorway is blocked by an accident and Paul, who has a particular hatred of traffic jams, decides to take the next exit and return to Paris on a B-road. "I just have to follow the GPS." They rush down long dark streets lined with ugly bourgeois houses, their shutters closed. Myriam nods off. The leaves of trees shine under the streetlights like thousands of black diamonds. Occasionally she opens her eyes, anxious that Paul, too, might have slipped into a dream. He reassures her and she falls back asleep.

She is woken by the blare of car horns. Eyes half-closed,

her brain still fogged by sleep and too much rosé, she does not at first recognize the avenue where they are stuck in traffic. "Where are we?" she asks Paul, who doesn't reply, who has no idea, and who is busy trying to understand what is blocking them. Myriam turns her head to the side. And she would have fallen back asleep had she not seen—there, on the opposite sidewalk—the familiar figure of Louise.

"Look," she tells Paul, pointing. But Paul is concentrated on the traffic jam. He is thinking about how to get out of it, perhaps by making a U-turn. He is at a crossroads where the cars, coming from all directions, are no longer moving. Scooters wind between the cars; pedestrians brush past the hoods. The traffic lights change from red to green in a few seconds. No one moves.

"Look over there. I think it's Louise."

Myriam sits up a bit in her seat to get a better look at the face of the woman walking on the other side of the crossroads. She could lower the window and call out to her, but she would feel ridiculous and the nanny probably wouldn't hear her anyway. Myriam sees the blonde hair, tied up in a bun at the back of her neck; she recognizes Louise's inimitable gait, agile and trembling. The nanny, it seems to her, is walking slowly, staring at the shop windows. Then she moves out of sight, her slender frame concealed by other pedestrians, disappearing behind a group of people who are laughing and waving their arms around. And she reappears on the other side of the zebra crossing, as if in the faded images of an old film, in a Paris rendered unreal by the darkness. Louise looks incongruous, with her eternal Peter Pan collar and her too-long skirt, like a character that has ended up in the wrong story and is doomed to roam endlessly through a foreign world.

Paul honks the horn furiously and the children are startled awake. He puts his arm through the open window, looks behind him and speeds down a side street, cursing loudly. Myriam wants to calm him down, to tell him that they are not in a rush, that there is no point getting so angry. Nostalgically she continues staring, until the last possible moment, at a chimerical, almost hazy Louise, motionless under a streetlamp, who appears to be waiting for something, at the edge of a frontier that she is about to cross and behind which she will vanish.

Myriam sinks into her seat. She looks ahead again, troubled, as if she had just seen a memory, a very old acquaintance, a childhood sweetheart. She wonders where Louise is going, if it was really her, what she was doing there. She would have liked to continue observing her through that window, to watch her live. The fact of having seen her on that sidewalk, by chance, in a place so far from their usual haunts, makes her desperately curious. For the first time she tries to imagine, in a corporeal sense, everything Louise is when she is not with them.

Hearing his mother pronounce the nanny's name, Adam, too, had looked through the window.

"It's my nanny!" he shouted, pointing at her, as if unable to understand that she might live elsewhere, alone, that she might walk without pushing a stroller or holding a child's hand. "Where is Louise going?" he asked.

"She's going home," Myriam replied. "To her own house."

Captain Nina Dorval keeps her eyes open as she lies on her bed in her apartment on Boulevard de Strasbourg. Paris is deserted this rainy August. The night is silent. Tomorrow morning, at 7:30—the time when Louise used to see the children every day—they will remove the police tape from the apartment on Rue d'Hauteville and they will begin the reconstruction. Nina has informed the investigating judge, the prosecutor, the lawyers. "I will play the nanny," she said. Nobody dares contradict her. The captain knows this case better than anyone. She was the first to reach the crime scene after the phone call from Rose Grinberg. The music teacher screamed: "It's the nanny! She killed the children."

That day, the policewoman parked outside the apartment building. An ambulance had just left. They were taking the little girl to the closest hospital. Already the street was filled with onlookers, fascinated by the screaming of sirens, the urgency of the medics, the paleness of the police officers' faces. Passersby pretended to wait for something; they asked questions as they stood in the doorway of the baker's or under a porch. A man, lifting his arm above the crowd, took a photograph of the building's entrance. Nina Dorval had him removed.

In the stairwell the captain walked past the medics who were evacuating the mother. The accused was still upstairs, unconscious. In her hand she held a small white ceramic knife. "Take her through the back door," Nina ordered.

She entered the apartment. She assigned each person a role. She watched the forensics experts working in their baggy white overalls. In the bathroom she took off her gloves and leaned over the bathtub. She began by dipping her fingertips into the cold, murky water, tracing ripples, setting the water in motion. A pirate ship was taken by the waves. She couldn't make up her mind to remove her hand; something was drawing her into the depths. She submerged her arm up to her elbow and then up to her shoulder, and that was how the forensics officer found her: crouching down, sleeve soaked. He asked her to leave; he was going to make an inspection.

Nina Dorval wandered around the apartment, Dictaphone pressed to her lips. She described the premises, the smell of soap and blood, the noise of the television and the name of the program that was on. No detail was omitted: the open glass door of the washing machine, with a crumpled shirt hanging out of it; the full sink; the children's clothes strewn across the floor. On the table were two pink plastic plates containing the dried-out remains of lunch. The police photographer took a picture of the pasta shells and the pieces of ham. Later, when she knew more about Louise, when she'd heard all the stories about the obsessively tidy nanny, Nina Dorval was surprised by the disorder of the apartment.

She sent Lieutenant Verdier to the Gare du Nord to meet Paul, who was coming back from a business trip. He'll know how to deal with the situation, she thought. He's an experienced man; he'll find the right words; he'll manage to calm him down. The lieutenant got there very early. He sat sheltered from the drafts of air and watched the trains arrive. He wanted to smoke. Passengers jumped down from a carriage and started running, in clusters. They probably had to catch a connecting train. The lieutenant watched as they passed, this crowd of sweating people: women in high heels, clutching their handbags to their chests; men shouting, "Get out of the way!" Then the London train arrived. Lieutenant Verdier could have walked to the carriage where Paul was sitting but he preferred to stand at the end of the platform. He watched the father of the dead children coming toward him, headphones covering his ears, carrying a little bag. He didn't move to intercept him. He wanted to give him another few minutes. Another few seconds before abandoning him to an endless night.

The policeman showed him his badge. He asked Paul to follow him, and at first Paul thought it was a mistake.

Week after week, Captain Dorval went over the course of events. Despite the silence of the nanny, who did not come out of her coma, despite the corroborating testimonies about this perfect nanny, she told herself she would find the flaw. She swore she would understand what had happened in this warm, secret world of childhood, behind closed doors. She summoned Wafa to police headquarters and questioned her. The young woman couldn't stop crying; she didn't manage to articulate a single word and in the end the policewoman lost patience. She told her that she couldn't care less about her situation: her papers, her work contract, Louise's promises, Wafa's naivety. All she wanted to know was whether she had seen Louise that day. Wafa said that she'd gone to the apartment in the morning. She'd rung the doorbell and Louise had half-opened the door. "As if she was hiding something." But Alphonse had run in. He'd slid between Louise's legs and he'd joined the children, still in their pajamas, sitting in front of the television. "I tried to persuade her. I told her we could go out for a walk. It was a nice day and the children would get bored in the apartment." Louise had refused to listen. "She wouldn't let me in. I called Alphonse, who was very disappointed, and we left."

But Louise did not remain in the apartment. Rose Grinberg is categorical on that point: she saw the nanny in the building's lobby, one hour before her nap. One hour before the murder. Where was Louise coming from? Where had she been? How long had she stayed outside? The police went around the whole neighborhood, showing people the photograph of Louise. They questioned everyone. Some of them—the liars, the lonely ones who make things up to pass the time—they had to tell to shut up. They went to the park, to the Paradis café. They walked through the covered arcades off Rue du Faubourg-Saint-Denis and questioned the shopkeepers. And then they found that supermarket CCTV video. The captain must have watched that recording a thousand times. She watched Louise walk calmly down the aisles until she felt sick. She observed her hands—her very small hands—pick up a carton of milk, a packet of biscuits and a bottle of wine. In these images the children run from one aisle to another, ignored by the nanny. Adam knocks some packets off the shelf; he bumps into the knees of a woman pushing a trolley. Mila tries to reach some chocolate eggs. Louise is calm; she doesn't open her mouth, doesn't call them. She heads for the till and the children follow her, laughing. They cling to her legs and Adam pulls at her skirt, but Louise pays no attention. Her irritation is betrayed only by a few little signs, spotted by the policewoman: a slight contraction of her lips, a furtive glance downward. Louise, the captain thinks, looks like one of those duplicitous mothers in a fairy tale, abandoning her children in the darkness of a forest.

At 4 p.m., Rose Grinberg closed the shutters. Wafa walked to the park and sat on a bench. Hervé finished his shift. It was at this time that Louise headed toward the bathroom. Tomorrow Nina Dorval will have to repeat the same movements: turning on the tap, leaving her hand under the trickle of water to test the temperature, as she used to do for her own sons when they were still little. And she will say: "Come on, children. Time to take a bath."

She had to ask Paul if Adam and Mila liked water. If they were usually reluctant to get undressed. If they enjoyed splashing around, surrounded by their bath toys. "There might have been an argument," the captain explained. "Do you think they might have been suspicious, or at least surprised, to be taking a bath at four in the afternoon?" They showed the father the photograph of the murder weapon. An ordinary kitchen knife, but so small that Louise could probably have partly hidden it in her palm. Nina asked him if he recognized it. If it was theirs or if Louise had bought it; if her act was premeditated. "Take your time," she said. But Paul hadn't needed time. That knife was the one that Thomas had brought them back from Japan as a gift. A ceramic knife, extremely sharp. Merely touching it to your skin was enough to cut into the flesh. A sushi knife, in return for which Myriam had given him a euro, to ward off bad luck. "But we never used it for cooking. Myriam put it in a cupboard, high up. She wanted to keep it out of the children's reach."

After two months investigating this woman, night and day, two months tracing her past, Nina started to believe that she knew Louise better than anyone. She summoned Bertrand Alizard. The man shook as he sat in the chair in her office. Drops of sweat ran over his freckles. He was so afraid of blood, of nasty surprises, that he stayed out in the corridor while the police searched Louise's studio flat. The drawers were empty, the windows spotless. They didn't find anything. Nothing but an old photograph of Stéphanie and a few unopened envelopes.

Nina Dorval plunged her hands into Louise's rotting soul. She wanted to know everything about her. She thought she could smash down the walls of silence within which the nanny had locked herself. She questioned the Rouvier family, Mr. Franck, Mrs. Perrin, the doctors at the Henri-Mondor hospital, where Louise had been admitted for mood disorders. She spent hours reading the notebook with the flower-patterned cover and at night she dreamed of those twisted capital letters, those unknown names that Louise had written down with the seriousness of a solitary child. The captain tracked down some neighbors from when Louise lived in the house in Bobigny. She asked questions of the nannies in the park. Nobody seemed able to figure her out. "It was hello, good-bye, that was all." Nothing to report.

And then she watched the accused sleep on her white bed. She asked the nurse to leave the room. She wanted to be alone with the aging doll. The sleeping doll, with thick white bandages on her neck and hands, instead of jewelry. Under the fluorescent lights, the captain stared at the pale eyelids, the gray roots at her temples and the weak throb of a vein beating under her earlobe. She tried to read something in that devastated face, on that dry and wrin kled skin. The captain did not touch the immobile body but she sat down and she spoke to Louise the way you speak to children who are feigning sleep. She said: "I know you can hear me."

Nina Dorval has experienced it before: reconstructions are sometimes revelatory, like those voodoo ceremonies where the trance state causes a truth to burst up from the pain, where the past is illuminated in a new light. Once you are there, a sort of magic can occur: a detail appears, a contradiction finally makes sense. Tomorrow she will enter the apartment building on Rue d'Hauteville, outside which a few bouquets of flowers and children's drawings are still fading. She will make her way past the candles and take the elevator. The apartment—where nothing has changed since that day in May, where nobody has been to fetch their things or even pick up their papers—will be the scene of this sordid theater. Nina Dorval will knock three times.

There, she will let herself be engulfed by a wave of disgust, by a hatred of everything: this apartment, this washing machine, this still-filthy sink, these toys that have escaped their boxes and crawled under the tables to die, the sword pointed at the sky, the dangling ear. She will be Louise, Louise pushing her fingers in her ears to stop the shouting and the crying. Louise who goes back and forth from the bedroom to the kitchen, from the bathroom to the kitchen, from the trash to the tumble dryer, from the bed to the cupboard in the entrance hall, from the balcony to the bathroom. Louise who comes back and then starts again, Louise who bends down and stands on tiptoe. Louise who takes a knife from a cupboard. Louise who drinks a glass of wine, the window open, one foot resting on the little balcony.

"Come on, children. Time to take a bath."